Zach Smith

ALI A DARWISH

authorHOUSE®

AuthorHouse™
1663 Liberty Drive
Bloomington, IN 47403
www.authorhouse.com
Phone: 1 (800) 839-8640

Published by AuthorHouse 08/12/2017

ISBN: 978-1-5462-0444-2 (sc)
ISBN: 978-1-5462-0443-5 (hc)
ISBN: 978-1-5462-0445-9 (e)

Library of Congress Control Number: 2017912511

CHAPTER 1

My life has been a series of vicious cycles—moments of extreme anger, uncontrollably sick love, depression, and unusual amounts of arrogance. I've shattered people's hearts. I've made millions of people experience the realities of a living hell, ruining their lives by using my gifts to tear down their intellects. No one is as arrogant as I am. Before you start to hate me, however, understand that I am trapped in the body of someone who cannot love. Well, that's not exactly true; I do love about five people. There have been good moments. I have singlehandedly taught a generation to fight their perceptions. I have taught people that life is about testing the intellect and challenging the mind. I have maneuvered millions of people to love me to the highest degree. My main crime against humanity has been low self-esteem, which has made me almost incapable of generally loving.

Oh dear Lord, spare me this misery. It is blinding me. There's a girl over there; she's been applying her makeup for the past twenty minutes. Everyone can see how ugly it is, except her. She definitely cannot see how ugly she looks. If she could, she would stop at once. She looks into the mirror obsessively, more fanatical about her looks than any individual should be. Bowing down to society's pressures, people are unable to live in their bodies without changing them. Oh God, now she is putting on her lipstick and smiling into her little handheld mirror, seeking her own attention. I cannot keep watching this girl! She is worsening my eyesight. Finally, I look away.

But the more I contemplate it, the more I think she may be conceited or an extreme narcissist. She may be seeking attention from her own self, since nobody else would ever give it to her. Maybe her life was damaged because her father or mother was not involved or present in her life. Maybe she is dating a guy who intimidates her or has some kind of emotional power over her and diminishes the person she could be. Or maybe I'm crazy. Maybe I'm the one who is obsessively seeking her attention because I find her attractive.

> Stop saying bad things about yourself; you know how great you are. You know how many good—actually, great—qualities you have, Zach. Do not be silly. You're not weird, and you do not need to seek the attention of anybody who is not nearly as great, smart, talented, or thoughtful as you are. You do not need to ever stoop that low again.

"Zach," says Albert.

"What's going on?" I reply, curious yet annoyed that he has disturbed my pondering.

"What school are you going to next year?" asks Albert. "You never told me. Do you even know yet?"

"Umm. Probably Floyd Elmer High School."

"I can't believe we're not going back to school together next year," says Albert. "That really sucks."

"Don't worry, bro. We will see each other around, and we can still play basketball on Fridays," I tell him. To be honest, I just want to stop his ranting about this so-called distance we will experience next year.

Albert's emotions are superbly intact and healthy, which is something I wish could be said about me. Or maybe I do actually have healthy emotions, but I've been convinced that they are not steady because I never express my emotions properly.

Our names are called by the store manager. I get up, take one last glance at that girl and, disgusted, walk away. I observe the way the floor is patterned, the dots in certain areas, the little flaws of the wood. I walk faster because Albert and the store manager, Rita, are far ahead.

Rita asks, "What can I help you with today?"

"We bought these two skateboards," I say. "We haven't used them, so we would like to return them."

"Here is the receipt," says Albert.

We all talk in such an orderly fashion. It's almost as if this conversation has been rehearsed to some degree.

"Okay, we can do that," says Rita, "since they look to be in store-quality condition. We can definitely do that without a problem." She hands us $220 in cash and the receipt, and we both at the exact same time say, "Thank you," and walk out of the store.

As I look around outside, I notice the birds and the way they all have this keen level of understanding. I love and hate it. It's a functional system, but on the other hand, it's a utopian society. Utopian societies are absolutely disgusting, in my opinion. People are wired differently. No one is built the same. However, these birds are part of a utopian society in such a way that allows them to live with each other. But the question I have in mind is whether these birds are actually all the same. There is a level of dominance that these birds display, even publicly. All animals, all forms of life, from plants to gorillas, display differences in personality and varying levels of dominance and influence. In a nutshell, is every creature similar—even the ones with a limited capacity? No, they aren't.

I admire societies that practice racial equality and religious equality. I was raised a Muslim, but I am not a practicing Muslim. I am not the type of Muslim who wakes up before sunrise every day to go to the mosque or who depends on God in times of hardship. I hardly ever pray or seek help from God. It may be sad, but that isn't the way I grew up. Throughout my life, I have been consumed by my own thoughts and vanity. When I feel vulnerable, I remind myself who I am, what my IQ is, and remind myself that I can change my vulnerabilities into strengths. I rarely feel vulnerable, but that doesn't mean that I am not constantly aware of my abilities.

As Albert and I get into the car, I have a fake emotional outburst, just obvious enough to ensure he notices. I puff and scratch my head exactly in the center, as if I'm upset about something. But he doesn't notice. I put my arm on the back of his seat as I reverse the car, which he notices as I continue to drive.

"Move your arm," he says. "Why are you grabbing on to the seat like that?"

I move my arm in a visually aggressive manner, making sure it's clear that I am unhappy. I wait until the light turns red. I lean my forehead on the steering wheel and blow air out of my mouth to show my agitation.

"What's wrong?" asks Albert.

I now have him trapped. "I can't talk about it," I say. "I'm not the type of person to look vulnerable. I don't usually show emotion like this." Inside, I am smirking.

"Dude, I am your best friend. Don't worry. I swear I'll never tell anybody."

"Okay, I'll tell you. You see, the issue is that I want to be iconic. I want to show everybody that I can be something great. I don't know why, but at times I doubt myself. I think that maybe I'm not intellectually capable of doing anything amazing. I sometimes feel like I'm not intelligent enough for anything." I am pleading to him, having picked every word to support my message. I use him to build my self-esteem, my confidence, my obsession with receiving applause for myself.

"Tom, you're the most intelligent person I've ever met," Albert says. "You're way smarter than I am. You have a brain unlike any person I've ever seen. Don't ever say anything vulgar like that again, bro."

"Thank you, man," I say in an appreciate tone. "That helps a lot. You're a great friend."

I drop him off and drive back to my house. While I'm driving, I am deep in thought. My natural response is to turn the music off, so it doesn't distract me or influence my thoughts. I drive more and I start shaking, hurting in my chest. I hurt more and more. I think about all the positive times I've had. But I am so blinded by the negative times, that I am unable to see the positive.

I remember everything. My memories are extremely visual—that stupid smirk on my teacher's face; being handed a paper that said I was leaving, that I can't live in Orlando, that I can't live in Florida. I am picked up later that day. I have no time to prepare for what is happening me. I am not allowed to feel emotions, because apparently I have the smallest part in the whole equation. What happened was a destruction of a marriage, and my little naïve self was never the focus. They never focus on me. They never tell me who I am. I live life wrong; I never feel anything. Emotions come and go. But, in my case, they rarely appear. When they do, I always blow them away, because I am in complete control of them. As I grow up I do not feel basic things. This damages me and, before I know it, my surroundings too. My refusal to be human is my greatest issue.

Had I stood up for myself back then, things would have been completely different. Had I been less of a coward or someone who cared less about his own wellbeing, things would have occurred differently. But for a long time I could not face who I was.

I grow into my teenage years and figure out that I am smart and capable. Nobody ever fed that to me when I was a kid, so I feed it to myself. And, as a result I become self-obsessed, a narcissist.

By the time I get home, that chest pain I experienced in the car slowly gets out of my system. What I do not know is that the pain I just felt is the beginning of something bad, something harmful, something that will change my entire life. This is the first time in my entire life that I feel truly connected with my actual emotions rather than a cover-up form of my emotions. Ironically, this connection to my emotions is derived from thought of how disconnected I am from my inner self. It is the first time I feel like I have exhibited raw, genuine, and complete emotion. This is what causes the pain in my chest, the knowledge that I have stored away so much emotion in my entire life that it slowly builds into an internal time bomb, in every single way—emotionally, physically, socially …

There have been times that I've listened to excessive hip hop music; making me feel inspired to create my own. I write something built on logic, because I have so little understanding of my emotions. I do not understand how to talk about my past, how to feel any type of compassion. My hip hop song is basically an instructional song about using logic to control your emotions. When there is a fight between the heart and the mind, always choose the mind; the heart carries emotions that will lead you astray.

I believe very few humans are able to completely control emotions the way I can. Very few humans are programmed to think, feel, and see the way I do, and have a perspective like mine.

Zach, you are the beginning of something so great;
someone who has never been seen before. You can
do things others would never dream of doing. Do not
feed off the failure of your surroundings.

I frequently have to tell myself not to become dependent on other
people's opinions. This is because I feel this lingering need to
manipulate others into complimenting me and seeing different
versions of me. I have a tendency adapt to each person's liking, very
rapidly and successfully, to ensure they see me in the exact light I
want them to see me.

———————❖◆◆❖◆◆❖◆———————

The next day I wake up at 11:26 a.m. I know that because I check
my watch every morning the second I wake up. Then I sit for about
twenty-five to thirty minutes, just gazing, examining the physical
structure of my bedroom. Why? I have no idea. Constantly, I have
this lingering feeling that I have overlooked something; something
that should be clear but I'm not seeing it. The wall is painted just
plain white, nothing distinctive, which I find aggravating. *How can
someone be so content with simplicity?* I think. Then it occurs to
me. It is my job to change the simplicity of these walls, of this whole
bedroom. It's as if someone has brought me a white canvas and some
paint. But if I am to alter this bedroom, it has to be in a way that is
remarkably out of the box, because I am a creative genius.

I get out of bed and walk around my room, slowly, so I can complete
my examination and figure out a precise plan for changing these
walls and making this room about something more than just the
color white. Maybe I should begin by looking at paint colors, finding
something I truly enjoy.

Then it occurs to me: I can make my room a setting for a complex
plan, with strings connecting blank paper all across the bedroom
and stacks of pens all over. I will use pens, because ink is not easily

erasable. And any thoughts I have, they clearly matter. If it seems wise or intellectual to me, that then it must hold value. I shouldn't be able to easily erase anything on the walls. I will write down my thoughts and plaster them all across the room. I will contain all my thoughts until I get home, so I can write and write. The strings will connect different abstract thoughts, making them compatible and creating solutions. *Man, this is the best idea I've ever had.* It is truly great, way better than some pointless paint job or hanging a photograph of a celebrity icon that I do not care about.

Later that day, I grow sleepy, so I decide that I need to sleep. Actually, I choose to sleep, because the word "decision" is a much more important word and has a larger meaning. So, I choose to sleep. First, I go to my sink, grab my toothbrush, apply the toothpaste, and brush my teeth. My toothbrush's forty-five-second timer goes off, so I stop brushing and rinse my mouth. Then I wash my face and go to bed. I lie there for about a minute, and I think about my sleeping habits. I always fall asleep incredibly easily. And I need to understand why. Studies I have read suggest that intelligent people find it much harder to sleep than other individuals. This is because they are so consumed by their thoughts. Maybe it is that I am just not programmed like the average intelligent person. It is as if there are guidelines for intelligent people, and one of them is an unstable sleeping condition. But simple things like this can't dictate intelligence. I conclude that thought and fall asleep before I can think about anything else.

———•——◆◆—◆◆—◆◆——•———

"Zach, you can't keep holding everything in!" my mom tells me. "Zach, you don't understand the danger it will cause you."

She always tells me that I shouldn't contain my emotions and bottle them up. I find that extremely peculiar, because I never feel as if I am bottling them up. It's not like I have emotions and refuse to release them. I just don't feel them, *What weird thoughts is she having?* I ponder. "I've actually been progressively improving in that aspect, and I always try to express them. I have been doing better. Trust me!" I want to stop her from yapping about something so worthless and annoying. *Why does she keep telling me all these weird things about my emotions? Why is there all this talk about my emotions lately?* Frankly, I am sick of it. I get extraordinarily agitated, but I don't let my mom see this, obviously, because I am very talented at containing my feelings and controlling my behavior.

"So … when does school start?" she asks.

"Umm, in two months," I reply. "Why don't you know that?"

"Why are you so agitated and aggressive?" She taunts me.

"I'm not. That's not true," I tell her. "I have to go upstairs and take a shower. Bye." I jog out of the room and go upstairs without allowing her to end the conversation properly.

She knows I am agitated. She can definitely tell. That's actually a great thing, something that I am incredibly happy about. I want her to see my agitation. For showing my agitation should ward her off, but only for now. She will come back, more aggressively, with her questions. She will tell me how I am harming myself by not letting any emotions out and how I will not live happily if I continue to do so. She really does think that it bothers me to hold them in. But damn, she could not be more wrong. I love containing my thoughts, because nobody should be able to hear them. If they do hear them, they may take them. Secondly, I do not share my thoughts because I go through thoughts super quickly. Solutions to problems appear so fast, I find myself not even needing to think about them. They just appear naturally. That's why I never go through crises. That's why everybody around me has nervous breakdowns, becomes angry, and yells uncontrollably, but I never do and never will. I never experience true anger without knowing exactly what I am doing, and that is honestly because I can problem-solve at a faster pace than many other people. When I feel agitation, it doesn't leak out unknowingly. I show my agitation by choosing my words and tone. There are never flaws in my behavior. When it comes to that aspect, I am truly flawless. I have to admit that to myself; after all, I am a narcissist.

I've been to Africa more than once, but this third time is different. I feel intimidated. I am on my way to Egypt, the country I visited when I was ten and eleven. Now I am fifteen; it has been four years since I last visited this country. It feels like an intellectual challenge, an adaptation challenge. To Egyptian's eyes, I am an "American," although my nationality is Egyptian, which makes it tougher on me, but I thrive off the challenge of fitting in. I do speak Arabic, exceptionally well considering I had not even seen the country or been in a predominantly Arabic environment until I was ten. Everything in this trip becomes a challenge as I try to adapt to my surroundings and appear to be a native Egyptian.

As I walk around, I feel nostalgic. I feel so alive. I see everything in a different light than I do when I am in America. As I talk to a few people, I notice the way they use words, the way they put their sentences together, their body movements, their intelligence. I notice the structure of the buildings—large, brown apartments with supermarkets or little shops on the bottom floors. I see people of all types, some of the whome have profound manipulation skills and use them to trick customers.

On the ride from the airport to our apartment, I watch Egyptians communicate and bargain with one another and take note of everything they do. My goal is to become just a notch superior to them when it comes to bargaining. I want to fit in and appear exactly like them. I am better able to adapt to the people around me than anyone else I know.

I look at the way Egyptians walk. They walk in several different ways. The loud and confident ones feel a great sense of belonging. The quiet and lonesome type shows a type of humility. There is a good mix of both types. There are others, but I focus on these two groups. I notice that many people swing their arms back and forth as they walk and look straight ahead, not around. That's probably because they live in Egypt, and nothing about it is intriguing to them. I take on these qualities. I take my arms out of my pocket and swing them back and forth as I walk. I look only about six to seven feet ahead of me and not all the way down the street and into buildings, as a tourist does.

At the snack shop on my street, I grab a mango drink. To ease my thought process, I contemplate everything in English. I ask the store owner, "How many pounds is this drink?"

"Six pounds," he replies, looking straight at me.

I return the favor and look straight at him. I pull out my wallet and say, "Take E£1.50 for it."

"No, brother, I cannot do that," he says. "I work hard for all this stuff."

I notice his use of the word "brother." He uses it to connect with my emotions, so I will give him the price he wants.

"Brother, we are both tired," I tell him. "I'm thirsty and just want a drink. C'mon man, let's do this for ..."

He cuts me off. "Okay, man, you can take it for E£4.50, but no more than that!"

"We worship the same God, brother," I fire back. "C'mon, don't do that." I use religion to combat his weapon of emotion.

"Four pounds, and that's final," he says firmly.

But I'm not leaving until I get it for E£3.00, maximum. "C'mon, uncle, don't do this, what if we say E£2.50. C'mon uncle." *Using the word "uncle" should definitely appeal to him,* I think. I smile my most intimidating smile, looking straight into his eyes. It's as if I am taking away his power.

"Take it for E£3.00, brother," he blurts out.

"Thank you very much, brother, may God bless you," I say. I accomplish my goal. I manipulate him all too well. But because I feel a little pity, I give him E£2.00 more, for a total of E£5.00—almost as much as his desired price.

I walk around Cairo with my mother and older brother, past souvenir shops with camels, pyramids, glass filled with colorful sand, carpets, paintings, rings, bracelets, other jewelry types, and etc. Naturally my brother decides he wants a souvenir. I am so annoyed by the thought of a souvenir—not because of the price, or the wait, or anything of that nature. I do not want an object to remind me of where I have been, because my mind does that already. Whenever I come to Egypt, I have a peculiar feeling— intimidating thoughts about being challenged, about belonging, about feeling a little less agitated—as well as powerful memories. I will always remember the way I feel when I am Egypt and connect the dots to the memories very quickly. My mind has always been able to connect dots rapidly.

As we walk, my mom asks me about Albert and how he is doing. "He should be doing all right," I reply. "I haven't spoken to him since we've been here," which is about twelve days.

"Isn't he your best friend?" she asks. Actually, that's a great question. I've made hundreds of friends, good friends, throughout the years— in Oklahoma City, where I live with my mom; in Santa Barbara, California, where my dad lives; and in Orlando, Florida, where I was born and mostly raised. I have many great friends because of my ability to understand people and see right through them.

But I answer the question as follows: "He can be considered one of my best friends, yes. I trust him more than any other friend I have. Yeah, I will text him or get back in contact with him." I add. She smiles and walks a little faster.

I love Albert, although he annoys the living shit out of me at times; he is emotional and difficult to withstand at times. Still, he is the most trustworthy person in my life and more like a brother to me than any other friend I have. Albert also makes it easy to feed my obsession. He knows me, well, there is no way to really "know me," but he knows me better than any of my friends. I appreciate the fact that he seems to know what I am capable of intellectually.

After three weeks in Cairo, we decide to travel to another Egyptian city—Alexandra. One morning, my grandmother calls a van to take us to a beach resort. We all pack up our bags, which is relatively easy because we arrived in Egypt with packed bags. We put our bags into the van and try to sit comfortably because this trip will be long, about three hours. The driver turns on the ignition, and we are on our way. Sitting in the car are the driver, my older brother, Muaz; my mom; my grandma; our maid, Raa'ida; and me, of course.

As we drive through the city on the way to the beach, Raa'ida gets a phone call. She answers the phone call immediately. It's actually super awkward that she answers it so quickly. Usually I wait about nine to twelve seconds, because anything less than nine seconds is weird, and anything more than twelve seconds is too much. I keep track of the seconds by looking at my Swiss-made watch. I am not a creature of habit, so I choose a different number of seconds each time. I am too creative to be a creature of habit; normal is a disgustingly boring mindset. As I am thinking about all of this, I hear her weep. I do not usually feel intimidated or angry but this is what I feel as she cries on the phone. Her emotions are agitating me. She is disturbing my peace, and one of my main desires is to have peace and no disturbances, unless I create them. I hate this little show she is creating . I hate it very much. I am so fixated on her tears that, for the first time in my life, I can feel my focus on my surroundings decrease. I am only able to pay attention on her weeping.

She closes the phone, and I quickly grab my earbuds and little music player to keep myself from hearing any of it. I try to make sure nobody notices me grab my earbuds because I don't want to appear heartless. But thankfully, my mother and grandmother are asleep. The only people awake are the driver, Muaaz, Raa'ida, and me. My brother isn't as good with women, or people, as I am, so he taps on my arm. I pause the music, take off the earbuds, look him straight in the eyes, and ask him, "What's up?" He tells me to ask Raa'ida what's wrong, and I refuse calmly. I tell him that I don't know how, because I truly do not know. He continues to insist that I ask her so I look at her, disturbed, and ask her what's wrong in the kindest tone I can.

She looks up, with tears running down her big fat cheeks, and says, "My grandma just passed away." It feels like a slap in the face. This is something serious. This isn't just a stupid emotional breakdown for no apparent reason. A death has occurred in her family and that is the reason for her emotional state. I try to show her I care, but I am incapable. I am so unable to do anything about her pain, I feel overwhelmed for the first time in my life. My entire leg shakes; it's a horrible feeling. Why do I feel this way? Why is this getting to me? Maybe it is because I am watching her deal with an issue that I have never dealt with. I am watching someone go through something I've never experienced or even truly thought of it. A small anxiety builds inside me because death has never occurred to someone I cared about. I manage to just tap her on the shoulder and look away. I'm shocked. But the more I think about it, the more I calm down. Soon, I am completely calm. My head stops hurting. I realize one thing:

if death happens to anybody around me, it would not affect me. I've been through so much anguish as kid that I no longer feel anything. I don't feel angry, and I am not sad. I'm just agitated at times; that is my only consistent feeling. My conclusion is that death will be like any other emotion I encounter: I will not feel it. It may damage me a little to see someone I truly love disappear, but I'm not scared of death, and it shouldn't have more than a mild affect on me.

——————◆◆◆◆◆——————

I am back in the United States of America. I am back in Oklahoma City. I get this weird feeling as I walk around; it's pretty annoying. It's a sense that there is a lack of diversity, everyone is uniform, and there are no differences in their personalities. It's the same exact feeling I had when I first arrived in Egypt. I walk through the airport and feel different from everybody. The time I've spent in Egypt has taken a toll on me. I figure this feeling should go away sometime soon, because it went away pretty quickly when I was in Egypt. As we walk through the airport we see all these shops. I'm hungry, and I do want to eat, but we would rather not eat in the airport, so we wait. I eat as much as I can. I am very picky, but when I find food that I like, like steak, I eat it relentlessly. The last time I ate good steak, I was in Santa Barbara with my dad, his wife, and my two half-sisters. My half-sisters are named after two twins in our family from a previous generation. Their names were Mia and Sarah. And as I think about them, I miss them. I miss them a lot.

When I fly back to Oklahoma City from Santa Barbara, I feel a tremendous force of guilt. I don't understand why I feel this guilt, but there is a good amount of it. Anytime I think about my little sisters, I feel like crying, like dropping down and weeping. I try to convince myself that it isn't my fault, that it is out of my power, that I can't control what happens, that I am too young. But thinking about them pierces my heart, and I am not emotionally capable of handling it. Those two girls are truly my weakness. I become drained if anyone ever says something bad about them. I will break the skull of anyone who says anything. I feel constant guilt for not being there with them, although, it is not my fault.

By nature, I am not a violent human being. I am calm and forgiving. I used to believe that I was incapable of feeling guilt. I used to believe I was mentally ill. I believed I was sociopathic. I was not able to feel empathy, guilt, or love. I used to wonder why I was so manipulative and did not care when I hurt people. I enjoyed breaking girls' hearts. I used to believe all these negative thoughts because my family would try to convince me I was heartless, narcissistic, brutal, and even sociopathic. But I stopped wondering why I felt this way when I realized those were traits others convinced me I had. In reality, I do feel guilt, I am kind, and I am definitely not sociopathic, although I may seem so at times. It's just that I am insanely more intelligent than everyone around me.

In case I have not done it right, let me introduce myself properly. My name is Zachariah, everybody calls me Zach. I am half Egyptian but was born and raised in the United States. My last name doesn't sound like an Arab name, because my father was a Muslim convert. A few years ago, he started to become less and less religious, and so did my mother, even though she was actually born into the religion. I am slim, tall, athletic. I was underestimated as a child; nobody knew I was as intelligent or talented. I am intelligent because of a natural motivation that exists in me. I used to read all day, every day, as a child. I had to, because it was an escape from my reality. My academics weren't always great. I taught myself to love math by reading my cousin Mark's textbooks obsessively. I was always highly independent.

I have a jawline and facial structure that makes girls fall for me. And then there is my personality. I can change people with my personality. I can make any girl crazy about me and any guy want to be my friend. But I get this feeling once I start to get close to a person. I immediately want to end the friendship or relationship. I act like the sweetest person to them; I seem like the greatest guy around, but I am the worst. I damage their self-esteem. I have been told multiple times that I shatter girls' hearts and that I neglect people. But frankly, I enjoy every minute of it. It is like a game to me, hacking into people's minds and controlling them; so well, that people never feel what I am doing to them.

I was once told at nine years of age that I am heartless. Who the hell tells a nine-year-old that he is heartless? As a young boy, I get scared anytime I feel any emotion, no matter how remote. I believe I am stupid, because my dad and brother have high levels of common sense, and they always make fun of my ideas. They tell me that I have no common sense whatsoever, that I am only academically smart and that is the only form of intelligence I exhibit. I work hard to adjust my thoughts, to think like them. I feed off the common sense of others around me, until I am smarter than everyone. My common sense increases greatly. My mind is sharp. I can connect thoughts and feelings. I can connect my perspective with words and moments. My thought process works at such a great speed, others are unable to catch up. At times, this makes me appear rude because I get agitated when I am at point Z while others are still at point A, barely moving onto point B. That sometimes makes it hard for me to deal with certain people, and I show it. Anytime, they tell me I act rude, I laugh, because I know their opinions are 100-percent insignificant. I completely understand how their minds function, and it isn't at my level.

———◆—◆—◆—◆———

The first day of school is hyped by everybody. It is fun to meet all former and new classmates, but it is also *school*. There are classes, schedules, and the overall feeling is the same. It's the people who really make me enjoy school. Albert is not with me in this school, and I miss him a lot, more and more every day. But I have friends in each of my classes, except P.E. I don't know anyone in that class.

At lunchtime, my friends and I stand around the math classrooms, which are the rooms closest to the lunchroom. Obviously, I am the center of attention; that is a given. I stand in the middle of the group, cracking jokes that could make anyone pee their pants. My jokes are clean. I can read every person around me, so I say things that will not offend anyone. For example, I don't use any cuss words. I make sure the topics suit the people listening to me. I put my profound intelligence to the best use. And every so often, I complain about something that is supposedly bothering me or any random thing, and get up and adjust my position or go somewhere else. I don't tell anybody to come with me. I just leave and sit in a different spot. And before I know it, every single person is following me, like a pack of hungry dogs chasing a man with meat. They don't see this as important, but I see it as control, controlling their positions. I have such an effect on them that they have to be around me.

Later that day, I am sitting on a bench by myself, and this kid named Wyatt sits next to me. I am not one to be rude, so I talk to him. I am very calm. I laugh politely with him, grabbing his shoulder so he feels a sense of closeness between us. He is a nice kid. It's just that I can see through him. He is very naïve, and he isn't insolent like a lot of other kids. I decide to befriend him. And from then on, we sit together most school days, waiting for the bus. When I am not there, he texts me or comes looking for me. We become pretty close friends.

We are always nice to each other and never argue. But one day, we are sitting together on the bench, and he is fooling around, and it gets kind of annoying. So I pull out my phone and start texting somebody. Wyatt keeps talking and talking until I am completely ignoring him. I don't know why he is being so odious, but I ignore him and don't snap at him. After he sees I am ignoring him, he says, "You don't hear anything when you're texting. It's like you become deaf."

And that's when I snap at him. That's when I show my intolerance. "I hear every single thing you say!" I yell. "I hear everything you don't say. I hear and feel everything everybody says, no matter what! Don't ever tell me that I don't hear something, even the slightest thing."

"Okay, man," he says, embarrassed and a little frightened. "I get the damn point. It's not that big of a deal."

I can tell this isn't a reaction he expects to me have. Nobody does. I am an outwardly calm person.

"No, no," I add. "Your incompetence is becoming increasingly exasperating. Do you not see it?" I make sure that is my last rude comment; then I plan to bring him back under my wing.

"All right, dude, I gotcha," Wyatt says. "I'll never do anything to bother you again. I'm sorry. I didn't mean it like that at all. You've become one of my best friends and possibly the only person that has genuinely been kind to me. So screw any problem we had. It won't happen again."

He is offering his apology. I accept it and make sure this is the last time we scuffle like that.

"It's cool, bro," I tell him. "Don't worry about it. I'm sorry too."

—•—••—◆•◆•◆—••—•—

Several months into school, the atmosphere calms down. Everything is quiet, and there is less commotion around the school. People are focused on their studies and on getting good grades. It is winter time. I am very friendly with every single teacher and all the students. I love my math teacher the most. But if there is one teacher I like the least, it is Miss Gausbi, my English teacher. Miss Gausbi is calm; in fact, she is unusually calm. She is quiet and peaceful. She studied psychology before she started teaching at Floyd Elmer High School. She apparently studied human behavior and is very good at evaluating it. This woman is a mystery to me. I can't see through her like I can other people, but I know one thing. She acts nicely toward me, but it is out of obligation, not genuine kindness. I know that I am not welcome around her. I can feel it in the way she did the little things. But I always try to stay away from her, because I know that there is more to her than meets the eye. There is something psychotic about her. That may be far-fetched, but I am adroit at reading people and seeing through them, and this is what I see.

Here is how it happens: I am in her class, making wisecracks, amusing the class and therefore amusing myself. I call on her. "Miss Gausbi?"

"Yes, Zach," she replies quickly.

I chuckle and smile before I say what I want to say. "It's funny, sometimes I think I have schizophrenia. I hear voices in my head talking to me. I hear things!" I emphasize the last sentence.

"Let me tell you something funny too," she says. "I think you have hypochondria." She tries to make a clever comeback. She probably feels offended—even though I didn't mean to offend her—because I have mentioned psychological disorders, and that is her specialty.

"What is hypochondria?" I ask, quite seriously.

"Obsession with the idea of having a serious but undiagnosed mental condition," she says.

I stay quiet. I am shocked. Why did she say that? Why did she say I have that? This woman has just humiliated me in front of my classmates. She puts me in a horrid light. This woman is heinous. I hate her. I can't even reply. So I just look at her and fake laugh. I hope this woman perishes off the face of the earth. She has serious issues. I'm great! There is nothing wrong with me! I never talk about any so-called "medical issues" around her. This is honestly the first time, and I've turned it into a joke. I feel an unparalleled need for revenge. I need to show her what she's done, even though nobody seems to notice. I will get her back, no matter how long it takes, no matter how deep I have to go to. But she will never make such an insubordinate statement like that again.

For the next couple of weeks, I don't think about what she did, because her opinion is completely insignificant. Her statement lacks sense, and I won't let anybody like that affect me—ever. One of the lines in a song I like is "A wise man once told me that holding a grudge is like letting somebody live in your head, rent free." Those words couldn't be more accurate. Once, I let people get to me, back when I was in a weaker state of mind. But now the thought of someone's opinion or comments having an effect on me is foolish. Nobody is able to control a mind as great as mine, for that is the true success of manipulation. So I start to forgive her and I end the grudge that I've been holding against Ms. Gausbi. I will never hold a grudge.

I walk around the doctor's office, looking for a spot to sit down in. The only vacant spot is near a man and his toddler. His toddler isn't crying, so I decide to sit next to him, even though my only other choice is to sit on the floor. I sit there quietly, knowing that I will be called within the next fifteen to twenty minutes. This doctor knows me like his son, at least that's what he says. He is a pediatrician, and I am only here because I feel extremely dehydrated. I have dealt with dehydration throughout various points in my life. My body dehydrates easily, especially when I'm doing a lot exercise, and I exercise a lot. I play soccer and basketball and work out every day. As I sit down, I turn my eyes toward father and son, who looks to be about eight or nine months old. The dad holds a tablet, which is playing a little cartoon, on mute. But the boy likes moving pictures, so he is satisfied. If he isn't satisfied, he will cry. I watch the way this father holds his baby—with pure love. I can feel it. The baby holds his dad's fingers, and his whole hand isn't even half as big as the man's finger. I am never captivated by anything emotionally, but this speaks to my emotions. I love it.

When I become a father, I want to become like this man. I want to be better than he is. I want to love my kid with everything I have, because I haven't been given much. I haven't been able to give any of my love to anybody or anything. I know I lack emotions at times and can be hard-hearted at times, but there will be no limit to my love for my kid. Love will flow from me. And I know every indication suggests it is too early for me to be consumed by these thoughts, but a child is the only thing I can love in that manner. I will raise my kid with understanding, never aggression. I will give him the choice of doing right or wrong; however, I will always teach him the ideology behind consequences. I will go anywhere and to any point if I ever lose him. I will sacrifice my life for him. I will anger him at least once, because I want to know how it feels to be even somewhat emotionally separated from him. Nobody really appreciates anything until it is gone. That is human nature and not the fault of any human. Humans become used to a certain lifestyle or a certain something and forget the true value of what they have.

My name is called, and the doctor tells me that I have to be on an IV throughout the weekend. We sit down and talk about a plan for healthier living, one that will stop me from getting dehydrated. That sounds like a dream come true. We talk about how much liquid I should consume daily and how to reduce my intake of simple carbohydrates. I promise to abide by his rules, but more important, I promise myself. I understand that a healthy lifestyle benefits me more than anyone else.

———————◆◆◆◆◆◆———————

I am one month into a new relationship and feel all sorts of complex emotions. It's like I am bipolar. I don't love her the way she says she loves me. I simply just admire her. Her presence doesn't bother me; it actually adds to my happiness. She is affectionate and highly intelligent. She can do things I'm not able to do. Her smile and her face glow. This girl isn't like the other girls I have talked to; she's different. I don't want to hurt her. I want to hold her and let her know I care about her more than anything. But I still have these thoughts: thoughts of how I don't love her. I merely admire her. That is how I feel about her.

Actually, the kindness is a feeling I used to have. It is absent now. And that is her fault. Alexa is just like everyone else; she has a low status in my eyes. In the eyes of a narcissist, that is, in my eyes, she is the worst one of all. I will make her suffer with unhappiness.

She has done nothing wrong. I'm actually on my seventh date with her; we are eating dinner, just her and me, at a pretty nice restaurant. I talk to her, looking straight into her eyes, as I usually do with girls, manipulating her emotions. I do simple, small things to make her feel the love that I don't actually have for her. The more I look into her eyes, the more I see her as disgusting. Looking at her is such an aggravating thought. I will plague her the way a narcissist does. And she will feel hurt in her chest anytime she even thinks about me. I will teach her a lesson—punishment for "loving me" and giving her emotions to me.

I start by putting my fork down suddenly and standing up. I walk around the table and hug her from the back. I whisper in her ear, "You're mine." and she chuckles. I grab her face softly, but with a grip, to indicate my confidence, and I whisper in her ear "You're all I need." She chuckles again, but this time it gets to her. This time she feels it, so I go back to my seat. We talk about our childhoods and how we were so innocent and cute. All of my stories are fake because my childhood was just a pile of misery. In the middle of laughing, I look her straight in the eye and wink, starting something cute between us. She winks back with that cute chuckle of hers, which made me fall for her at one point.

"You know, Zach, I trust you so much," she says. "I'm being completely honest. I don't care if you talk to any other girls as friends. It used to bother me a lot, but I don't care about it anymore. In the past, I used to jump, because I was scared to lose you. But now I trust that nothing bad will happen. You're unlike any guy I have ever met. There's this notion of kindness that you have, like you can understand me very well. It's like you can read me, so you alter everything you do to make me happy. I think you're amazing." She smiles as she says the last part. I let her finish as I usually do, thinking about everything I hear.

She is so wrong and right all at once. However, she feeds my obsession, i.e., my desire to hear great things about myself. She makes me happier than I was before I figured out I want to dismantle her heart. She says she trusts me; oh my, is she wrong! She says she doesn't care if I talk to girls because she trusts me. She is wrong to say that. However, I will feed into it when I respond to her. I am unlike any guy she's ever met. She is correct about that. I'm unlike any guy anyone has ever met. I don't see things in terms of branding; I see the little details surrounding things, and that's thanks to my low latent inhibition. I'm more intelligent than any other guy she has ever met too, judging by my IQ and my own knowledge of what true intelligence is. I am kind, as she says, but at the oddest times and rarely toward a girl. She says, "It's like you can read me, so you alter everything you do to make me happy." This is completely correct, to the point that I celebrate that opinion far longer than I usually do—maybe twenty four-hours. I can read her completely and effortlessly, and that's the greatest weapon I have against her.

"Aw … That's the sweetest thing ever. I trust you too. You mean so much to me. And I definitely try everything I can to make you happy, because you're all I need." I reply with a smile, giving her the exact answer she wants. If only she could see how amateurish she looks.

After we finish eating and complimenting each other, I walk over to pull her chair out, so she can get out effortlessly.

"Oh, you're such a gentleman, Zach," she says. When she stands up, I kiss her cheek, right next to, but not directly on, her lips because she's just eaten. "I'm so lucky, babe," she says.

"Oh, well, I'm luckier," I say, smiling. "You're beautiful in every way." I can sense her attraction; I can read her, just like she said I can. I guess we do share a thought: we both believe I can read her.

She gets into my car, and I drive her home. She lives only two minutes away from the biggest mall in Oklahoma City. She lives in a rather rich area. I think it is a magnificent place to live. I also live in a rich area, but sometimes I forget that my family has money, because I am so consumed by my thoughts. I don't see having money as a virtue. Of course it's a great thing to have. But even being slightly consumed by materialism and money will undeniably change a person.

Alexa distracts my thoughts by saying, "What do you want to be when you grow up? As your profession, you know?" She's asked a conversation-blooming question. That's a question into which I have put hundreds of hours of thought.

"I think about that every day, actually," I say, seeming to hesitate. "I want to do clinical human behavior trials. I love the human mind, and all I want to do is get to the bottom of how it works, if that is even remotely possible." This time, I am not just feeding my obsession; that is actually my aspiration.

"You're highly intelligent," she says. "I love that about you, Zach. You are going to be great at anything you do. I promise you that; your ambition just flows through the air." This time I am not looking for her to say that, and I think deeply about what I want to be, about whom I want to be as a man.

She steps out of the car. I kiss her goodbye, and she walks into her house. Before she turns her head for the last time, I see something that makes my heart sink. A tear streams down her face as she walks away. I sit in the car, motionless. I can't figure out where that tear came from, and the scariest thought is that perhaps it is from love. I can't move. I can't drive away. I can't stop thinking about that tear on her cheek.

What happens when guilt affects your regular thoughts? What happens when you wrestle with your conscience? This is what happens! Who does Alexa think she is, trying to tell me to read her? She dropped that tear right before she walked away from me. She is sneaky and a master manipulator of my emotions. Maybe she's read me, is that it? She's read the master of manipulation? The one with a level of intelligence that is unmatched by any other individual? Did she trap and manipulate me? Maybe she can see what I want to do to her emotionally—that I want to take her heart apart, shatter it, and put it back together on my own terms. There could be so many reasons for that tear. But she cannot be smarter that I am! I control her! Maybe this fear of such a simple thing, like a tear, is me falling in love. But no, that can't be true, I don't fall in love. What a vile thought. No, I don't love; she is simply a nuisance. I need to know exactly where that tear came from.

I call her the minute I get home, and she answers right away. Again, this is something I see as pretty weird. I always wait a number of seconds before answering a call. I say, "Right after you left my car, you turned your head, and I saw a tear glistening in the street lights. There was a tear falling down your face! Where did that come from? Why were you crying?" I get louder and louder as I continue to speak.

"I can't tell you," she responds. It will sound stupid, Zach. I just can't, I'm sorry."

"I can't play this back and forth game with you. I need to know. Please, tell me," I say calmly, I am putting pressure on her to tell me.

"I can't tell you," she says, and adds abruptly, "Also, I've got to go. Bye, Zach."

"Whatever," I say. "Bye." I am angry and feel helpless. But she is not worth me feeling like this, and I won't let one damn facial expression have control over me. I will suppress this emotion, as I have the ability to do. She is not deserving; nobody is. I don't want to feel dreadful, and this feeling needs to stop now. I can feel my chest being cleansed; that feeling goes. I'm not angry; I don't feel hurt. Nothing is bothering me. Unlike most humans, I have an ability to control all thoughts, feelings, and emotions.

Alexa is an emotional wreck. If she is not a fully formed emotional wreck yet, I will expose her as one soon.

We walk through the school hallways. I walk in her direction, but in front of her. I talk to every girl I see, and she notices. Let's see how far this so-called "trust" that she has in me will take her. I'm aggravated at the world at this point. I feel betrayed by so many people and, I swear, I'll take it all out on her.

Tracy is walking in the hallway. She is the one girl I know that has liked me consistently for years. I go up to her. "Hey, Tracy."

"Hey, Zach."

"You look really good today," I tell her. "Like not to be weird or anything, but you just look superb." I smile when I say "superb," using the smirk that shatters hearts. I use that smirk to tear people apart; throwing it in her face.

"Aw … Thank you, Zach. You're the sweetest." She grabs me and hugs me. I can see Alexa walking back and forth between the bathroom and the window. She acts like she isn't looking at me, but she is. It's very obvious. I whisper in Tracy's ear while she's hugging me; I whisper in Tracy's ear as I look straight at Alexa, into her two eyes.

"You're the cutest, Tracy," I whisper. "I wish you were mine."

She says into my ear this time, "Zach, you don't know it, but I am for you." She pulls out of the hug and kisses me, halfway cheek and halfway lips. I put my hands on her shoulders, still while looking straight at Alexa. I then push Tracy away, saying, "Tracy, don't do that."

"Don't do what?"

"Don't kiss me. I'm sorry. I have to do something. I'll catch up with you later, all right?"

"Yeah, sure, whatever, Zach."

I've exposed Tracy. I've made her look bad in front of Alexa, even as I look into Alexa's eyes. She doesn't know it, but I've made an example of her. It's like in the movies where the bad guys kill one hostage to teach the others to toe the line.

For days, I talk to other girls, look them in the eyes, give them my special smirk. And each time, I tell Alexa that it isn't a big deal, I didn't mean to do anything wrong, in fact, I didn't do anything wrong. I want to hurt her sooner than later. But we calm manipulators have great amounts of patience. I take her to a park where we can walk around peacefully. Alexa says, "Zach, babe, I want to sit down" and points toward a black metal bench. I walk over and read "In memory of Jonathan Kaimart and Rhonda Willyosin." What a pair of weird last names! We sit down, and I put my arms around her; she lies her head on my chest.

"I don't like the girls you've been talking to," Alexa says. "I do trust you. But it makes me feel very insecure and hurts me." She sounds stressed out. I've taught her to always tell me what's on her mind and not beat around the bushes. I don't like people to throw subtle or unusual hints at me, and she understands that. I want to know to what degree what I am doing is hurting her. Even though I already know, I want to hear it from her mouth.

"It hurts you? It really does?" I say, sounding both clueless and empathetic.

"Yes, it hurts me a lot, Zach. Please don't do that anymore."

"Alexa, baby. I won't do it anymore. I'm sorry. You don't have to worry," I assure her. Then I kiss her, and we get up to walk more.

For about a week and a half, we walk around together during school hours, looking like a couple. I give her such a relaxing sense of security and loyalty during this week and a half. I put my time and energy into making her feel secure, until it is time to make my last move. I walk her almost to her class, but not all the way, like I normally do.

She asks. "You can't take me to class all the way?"

"I have to talk to someone about something right away," I tell her. "I'll see you later on."

"Okay, bye," she says, with a hug, putting her arms around my neck. That's the last time she'll ever hug me like that. I then speed walk about fifteen feet and go up to a girl named Allison.

"Alli! What's up!" I say enthusiastically. I'm not necessarily enthusiastic about seeing her, but about what's going to happen next.

"Zach! What's going on with you,?" says Allison.

Alexa sees me grab Allison, a little above her wrist and watches us walk a little. I hug Allison and rub my hand in a circular motion around her back, all the while looking straight into Alexa's eyes.

"Oh my God, Zach, you're being super touchy today!" Allison has a gorgeous smile on her face. But I'm more focused on Alexa's face.

"I haven't gotten a good kiss in a while," I tell Allison. "I'd love to have one."

"I can't do that, Zach," she says. "We aren't together."

"I meant on the cheek. Just a friendly one of course," although I actually mean a kiss on the lips. I just don't want to sound like someone that jumps from girl to girl.

"Yeah, I can give you a friendly kiss," she says, smiling. She plants a kiss on the right side of my face. I look up at Alexa, and I can sense what she is feeling. She knows I've betrayed her. It hitting her all at once. She's figured out my plan. She knows I did everything on purpose to get to her in this exact situation. She knows it all now. I look her in the face, and I wink, turn my face, and walk away. I hear the noise of something shattering—her heart breaking into many pieces. I've accomplished just what I wanted, effortlessly.

It's been about two weeks since I broke Alexa's heart. I hear the noise of it breaking every day. I am not one to feel guilt. Why am I feeling it? Is it normal for something so amateurish and simple to break my heart the same way I broke hers? I think about it every single day. Do I love her? No I don't love her. I don't even like her. Any form of attraction I felt for her declined abruptly the day I chose to manipulate her. I need to break this down until I figure why I've done such a vulgar thing. Why did I decide to break her in that way?

I know why I did that to her; suddenly, it's all clear. Thoughts flow to me rapidly, like water gushing from a dam. I realize that it is the fault of my surroundings, the people around me that have brought me up. They has convinced me that I love to torment the people around me, and I believe it. I feed into it. I need to hurt people, but why? It is because I am talking to my childhood. This whole time I've been subconsciously talking to my childhood. I want to hurt my childhood, I want to get it back for what it's done to me. But there's always a need also to hear the authentic voices from my childhood. I want to know if its points were valid when it successfully convinced me that I have a merciless nature. Or am I supposed to appreciate my childhood?

It makes me happy to hear Alexa's heart shatter. *No, Zach, you're listening to your childhood again. That's what it wants—to tell you that you are sick, to convince you that you lack humanity. And you're listening to it, Zach.* I feed into what it tells me, but it is wrong. I am not heartless. I am kind but furtive. My creativity, not my childhood, has made me who I am. My mind has taken me on this path. I feed off of moral dilemmas, and when they come my way, I know what I am doing. I choose the wrong option more often than I should. I choose the wrong option to feed into the childhood that scarred me.

No! Never again will I say that it scarred me. That is a lie, a filthy lie I've lived with all my life. I will not let anything have power over me the way my childhood has. I want to hurt the people who tell me I am heartless. Actually no, that was the past. My childhood no longer has any power over me. My childhood is the reason for my high intellect, and I am grateful for it. I thank the childhood that I've always despised. Sometimes, your greatest enemy is your greatest teacher.

<hr />

We've both grown up so much, intellectually and physically, Albert and I. He is no longer annoying. We've gotten older, and I see him as a young man now.

We are sitting on a park bench. Albert is yelling out loud, agitated at his mother. He looks up in the sky, as if reading the lines to his next moment of rage. "I hate the way she always acts like I am some kind of infant," he says. "I am not. I'm more mature than most adult men that I know." As distraught as he is, he is the healthiest person I know, emotionally. He is able to control his anger, and let it out at the right time. His emotions are so intact. When he lost his little brother, Sean, he cried for days, months. But he was the manliest person I knew, even when he had to cry.

He always tells me, "Zach, I learned to celebrate the life he had more than mourn over his death …Zach, do you know what it's like to be angry about what the world has done to you? It took away the one thing I always wanted to do, love my brother and grow up with him."

Albert lives with his mother and stepfather—his stepfather and Sean's. He hates the very thought of his mother but always pays her unconditional respect. He can have a hard time loving others; Nevertheless, he loves me. He loves me like he loves no other person. It comes to a point where we no longer see each other as friends but as brothers. In him, I see everything I am not. I see a man who can change people for the better.

Sometimes, though, I see a tool, and I use it. Sometimes, I see a man who can feed my obsession in the best form. But having those thoughts also hurts me at times. When I see him, guilt surrounds me. It swells up my throat and stabs my chest. I never want to upset Albert. I don't know what true love is, but I know I will always appreciate Albert, for the man he is, for the brother he is to me.

"It'll be okay, man," I tell him. "I swear, it'll be okay. Your mom loves you. Remember to always see the good in every situation. Don't ever close your eyes to the gifts around you." I playfully punch his shoulder.

Sometimes, Albert looks at me and says, "You motivate me more than my own parents do. You're my drive. I have so much respect for you, man." And when he tells me that, I am puzzled. I am perplexed. Albert is a special being, a righteous man in the body of a boy, and yet he's expressing *his* pleasure at knowing *me*? He says he respects a person who isn't half the man he is—a person who suppresses his emotions, and who exhibits mild psychopathic traits. Why do I think of myself in this way? *No, Zach, don't think like that! There is a reason he respects you.* He respects me because my brain functions on a different level. My brain system is masterful. I am a genius. I can't convince myself that a sickness lives inside me. There is no sickness. It's just that my mind works in complicated manner. I'm a narcissist; self-love is all I have. I can't let a single falsehood communicate with me. Albert should respect me, and he does, because it is foolish for him not to. He has to respect the person with an attitude that one cannot ignore, who breaks people mercilessly. Oh God, don't say that last part. It is happening again. I believe what people say about me. I knock myself down when I don't deserve it.

I turn around and look at him. "Albert, I want to write a book. I want to write about the things I believe. I want write about selfishness and heartlessness. I want to write stories about how damaging it is to convince a young boy that he is selfish. How can people tell a boy that he is heartless, that he lacks emotions, that he has the mind of a psychopath?"

"Damn, man," says Albert. "It'll be all right. I can tell you're bothered. You dealing with anxiety or something? It'll be okay, bro." He has a calming tone. I don't get anxious; if only Albert knew how capable I am, how alert my brain is. I don't get anxious. Wait, no! I have been anxious for the past seven months. I have been shaken, guilty. But that is the fault of my childhood, the shattering feelings my childhood gave to me. But I have told myself that I will no longer talk about it or think about it. I will not let one thing control my entire life; nothing should control a brilliant human mind. I do not think about my childhood anymore, so I regret what I've said to Albert. I wish I hadn't told him that.

"It's fine, Albert," I tell him. "I'm good, man. I'm not thinking about anything. I don't feel that way, I've just been reading about anxiety a lot, and seeing a lot of people with it. I do want to write a book about it one day, in exclusive detail."

"Okay, bro," he says, "and I hope you stay dedicated and gain much success."

———•——••—•••—••••—•••—••—•———

I walk through my neighborhood all alone at midnight. My neighborhood is among the safest in Oklahoma City. I look down on my pedometer, panting; I've jogged about three miles. I'm tired. I don't know why I run like this; I have no idea. I decide to run late at night without any conscious decision making, I just take my Bluetooth earbuds and music player, and jog out of the house. I don't know how I feel about this; my reasoning and feelings are so vague. Lately, I have become intolerant of these mood swings. What happens when someone who can control everything starts losing his touch? Do you know what it means to control, to govern your own thoughts and emotions, to govern the feelings of others? But now I am losing my touch. I cannot be who I was. I run. I shake at times. I hurt at times. What is making me like this? I wish I knew.

I am in first grade, and my teacher says, "Write down a complete sentence on this paper, Zach."

All I can write is "the fox ran." Every time I am asked, I write the same sentence.

"No Zach, you can't do that. Stop writing that sentence. Have some creativity!"

So I write "the dog ran," and the teacher gets agitated. She grabs the papers of all the students and shows me their sentences. There is creativity all around the room, sentences like "The glass broke on the floor" or "Dennis ran through the hallway."

The teacher says, in an aggressive tone, "You're not stupid. Use your creativity. Why can't you be like the others?"

She remains my teacher through the third grade, which is when I leave Florida. She is the one who tells me that I'm leaving for Oklahoma. I will never forget her smirk, when she smirks and makes me read from a paper: *Zach, you are leaving this state. You will not live here again.*

These memories play in my head, but they're not just playing, they're destroying me. Why is this happening to me? Why can't I be myself? Why am I falling apart? Maybe, I do just keep all my feelings inside.

I walk around slowly, because I'm analyzing everything—the behavior of others, the way they are, how they react to little things. Everything intrigues me; everything. I think about cars, and those thoughts lead to many other thoughts and very rapidly. My mind starts adding and subtracting thoughts too fast, until I remember sitting on a plane looking at the neatly uniformed flight attendant making an announcement. She tells us that we have to put our oxygen masks on and help ourselves before helping anyone else in case of an emergency. I recall her saying that we had to help ourselves first before anyone, even a baby. I don't understand why one would help oneself before helping the toddler nearby in need of air, so I ask the attendant why that was. She tells me that if someone is unable to put his own mask, that person may pass out, making him incapable of helping anybody. The more I think about that, the more I realize how much it pertains to everyday life. For one to be generous and help others, one must become selfish first. This is a general formula for life. People need to understand that there are many reasons for a person to be selfish.

I walk around every day and look into the eyes of a woman who believes I am heartless. I tell her, "One day I'll convince you that

I'm not heartless." She does not believe me; she does not think it is possible. Sometimes, I am unable to help others, because that will knock down my stability. So I've stopped caring what people say about me and about who I am. It doesn't concern me anymore, and I don't spend time thinking about it. I can't prove to anyone that there are kind emotions in my chest if they don't see them. People see my emotions and my kind heart; it is her loss that she cannot. She is a critical reason for my callous upbringing. Callous may be a harsh word, but that's the only word to describe what has been done to me. I despise her at times. But there are days when I love her with all my heart, and those days are more frequent than the days when I hate her. She is my mother after all.

I sit in my room, shivering; the temperature is freezing in my house for some reason. It is winter in Oklahoma, and though our air conditioning is still on, I'm cold. I don't want to get up or do anything. I want to lie in bed, motionless. I'm a human being who bleeds ambition, but right now, I can't think of anything I want to do. I just sit here, slumped in bed.

The cold is evil. This may be the way some of them see me—cold, the killer of ambition, the killer of all. I want to know why the people who shaped my childhood have such a ruthless view of me, as if I completely lack empathy. I know I feel it though, I know they're wrong, because guilt stabs me in my chest continuously. I've been having these thoughts lately, routinely.

I tell myself that the cold is powerless; I feel lazy and incapable, but I will not let that limit me or my pursuits. Success is what I want and what I will work toward until I can't anymore, until I shrivel and can't stand up, until I achieve it. Otherwise, I will die trying.

I stand up and analyze the thought Wall I've built. I document on this wall every thought or feeling I've had in the last seven months. I want to know how to let out all these thoughts that I keep inside. I want to be different. I string together all thoughts that are somewhat related on the wall. I use it to solve my problems and to link everything together. I look at the anger side of the wall. Whenever I feel angry, I write down exactly how I feel and why I feel that way.

For example, recently I was so enraged, all I could write on the wall was: *Heart shaking. Anger. Hatred. Heart beating rapidly. Fear.* That's all I could express. It had not been a crisis; it was just a few moments of anger.

Whenever I feel angry, I don't exhibit aggression or any other physical reaction. My anger causes me to devise plans, well-thought-out, unsympathetic plans. I put my mind into a zone of complete patience, and there is not much anybody can do to influence me to release my anger. If somebody bothers me, I want to tear him apart and make him understand what he's done to me. But luckily, I very rarely feel this way; I very rarely want to humiliate anyone. I'm forgiving and thoughtful. There is not much people can do to encourage me to hurt them.

As I look at my anger side of the wall, I return to the time I wrote that message. Furious, I'd strung my feelings together with vulnerability. I didn't want to hurt Mark, the person who had angered me, because I loved him with all my heart. But I wanted to teach him vulnerability. I wanted to teach him a lesson because of what he did to me. I wanted to teach him that he couldn't live without me. I built up a plan to get the people in his inner circle to hurt him and take him apart. My goal was to remind him how much he needed me and that if he ever angered me again, the feeling of loss would paralyze him.

Everybody around Mark feels loved but also skeptical. People are afraid that he uses them. They believe he isn't emotionally intact. Mark is my older cousin, he is more like my brother than my cousin. He is kind, but I can see through his heart and can see how much he plagues the people around him. That's how I knew how everybody else felt about him, because I felt that way. Perhaps they aren't able to admit it to themselves.

I decide to capitalize on their inner distrust of Mark. These people are his close circle of friends, whom I've grown to know very well. I want to help them release their distraught feelings. I'll used them all to hurt Mark emotionally, so he will remember me.

Noah is Mark's work partner and one of his friends. They own a Chrysler dealership on the outskirts of the city. One day, I am at Mark's house, and Noah is there too. Mark is in his bedroom, agitated, apparently for no reason. His problem is that he gets angry at the most imbecilic things. I take Noah aside in the kitchen and talk to him. I begin my well-planned manipulation process.

"Noah, are you okay?" I ask him, seeming genuinely worried.

"I'm good," he replies. "Every day is a good day, man. Why? Do I look upset?"

"No, no. I'm just asking, man. It's no big deal."

"Oh, okay. Thanks for asking, Zach."

"You're welcome, Noah. Hey, man, I've been meaning to ask you something. I've been kind of wondering, I don't mean to be rude or anything. I'm just curious."

"Go ahead," says Noah. "Don't be afraid to say anything. It won't offend me."

"Okay, man. Just please don't tell anybody that I told you this."

"I promise I won't say anything. You know I won't," he says, curious.

I'm stalling a bit for two reasons—first, to sound innocent so he will never trace the pain that he is about to inflict onto Mark back to me, and second, to intensify his inquisitiveness. "Mark does this thing where he undermines your position," I tell Noah. "That's just how I feel about it. I don't think he understands your contributions at the dealership. We both know how successful you are at the dealership and your effectiveness at selling the Chryslers. I've been analyzing everything, and it's like he has this irrational sense of entitlement. But he doesn't do this on purpose; he's doing it unknowingly." I project sincere concern.

"Really, man?" says Noah. "That means a lot coming from you, especially because I know how close you two are. But why do you feel this way? I don't understand where this is coming from." He seems slightly confused.

"It's just my perception of things; that is just how I see this situation. He talks about the dealership as if he is the only owner. He seems to want to take control of it himself. I know he is the owner, but you are the other owner. It isn't only under his name."

"Oh, okay, I understand," Noah says. "I see what you mean. You are right. He does have that sense of entitlement. Don't worry I won't say anything to anybody about this." And I believe him when he says he won't say anything. I know exactly how much he can keep inside. And I also trust that he will give enough hints to make Mark feel betrayed. That is my objective.

I start to read Noah's body language and observe his actions. He is frustrated, although he tries to keep it in. When Mark is talking to him, Noah lowers his head and covers it with his arms. He shows a substantial amount of carelessness about what he must say. When he's asked about this behavior change, Noah tells Mark that he is tired. He keeps repeating, "I'm tired. Stop asking!" His tone gets more aggressive, the more Mark questions him, which Mark does about seven times before he finally gets irked.

I don't want Mark's pain to be that slight. This is just the first step of my manipulation process, my pain-infliction process. So I hurry to stop this little thing that is going on. I don't want Mark to think that I have his back, so I walk into his room and call Noah. I give Noah a pep talk about staying calm and kind. But the advice I give him is not what I want, which is for him to keep it in until his frustration boils over, and he just pops on Mark. When he does, Mark will be in dire need for someone to be there for him, but this time it won't be me. Then he will understand how much he needs me. I can read his entire book of emotions, and I know all his weaknesses and pressure points. I will build on the blueprints of his personality. I can't wait until he feels what hits him. He's angered the most dangerously angry person. He's angered a person who can singlehandedly take people apart.

I want to anger him; I want him to feel vulnerable. I have these frantic thoughts. What happened to the person I was before all of this anger? I had been peaceful, unaffected. I did not care about other people's opinions. I didn't dwell in my own anger. But lately, a thing has formed inside of me, and it has grown rapidly. It is a lack of fear. I do not fear my thoughts or myself anymore. I used to have an internal fear, which I believe every person should have. I never would have entered a realm of arrogance like this. I never had effusive, proud thoughts. My mindset wasn't always characterized by a constant inability to accept the intelligence of others. Manipulation was not a plan that I would have devised. Now, I feel the urge to take down my family. I want to cut into their hearts with my perseverance. I want to hurt them, because I hurt, which is a new and surprising realization for me. I always believed I didn't hurt, that I couldn't feel emotional pain. I've come to realization of my growing pains because I don't fear my thoughts anymore. I'm no longer able to suppress my thoughts; I'm no longer able to stop myself from taking people down one by one.

My ignorant family undermined me; they convinced me that I am stupid, unintelligent. They said I had sociopathic traits. But I can't be stupid, because I am more intelligent than any of them. I can't be both stupid and a sociopath who can control a system. I am more than the average creative genius. My memory is profound. I admire success and fanatically work toward it. They don't know far how my intelligence reaches. They will find out, though. I'm going to revolutionize whatever I do, and they will sit there in awe while I splash their own blood across their faces. I will terrorize them. I will make an example out of each of them. I want them to feel the dent they have created in me. I will manipulate those around me, obsessed now with more than just a desire to get praise from others. I feel vengeful. I want to show them what they have done to me. I will repay them with my own blood and hurt. I will petrify their spirits. I will not quit until I take away their regular human abilities.

I am lying on a king-sized bed in my room. I snap myself back into thoughts of Mark and the vulnerability he will feel. I want him to be anxious, to have a type of nervous breakdown. I continue with my plan.

I play late-night basketball. My basketball runs are routine. I go to the gym with three or four friends, even on school days, from 11:00 p.m. to 1:00 a.m. We play a lot of basketball and have the whole gym to ourselves. I am not the best on the court, talent-wise, but I am the toughest to beat, mostly because of my nasty defensive strategies. I intimidate my oppoonents to limit their offensive abilities. I play basketball ruthlessly, because I cannot let others beat me without putting up a heart-aching fight. I play with overloaded aggression and earn praise each time I play. Thirsty, I go to the bench to drink some water, and my phone rings. It's Noah. I wait about nine seconds to answer. "Hello" I say.

"Hey! What's going on?" says Noah.

"I'm just playing some basketball. What about you?"

"I just called you to talk about Mark," he says.

"What about him?"

"I've noticed what you mean, how oppressive he is. He doesn't include me in conversations about the dealership. It's like I don't exist, and he's the sole owner. But it belongs to both of us."

"Well, man," I tell him. "Give him a hint. Let him know." He might as well, since he sees and feels it. It's a feeling that he has now. I'm not convincing him of anything.

"Okay, man," says Noah. "I'll try to get him to see how entitled he sounds."

"All right, bro," I say. "Bye."

"Bye," says Noah.

Three days pass. Mark is about to lose it over Noah's behavior. Noah has made his disconfort with Mark obvious. Mark chooses to confront him about it. I have encouraged Noah to bottle up his feelings, so that when Mark pokes him, he explodes.

"I am sick of you acting like this," says Mark. "Stop it. You aren't productive at work, and you are acting unusually."

"Do you know who I am?" asks Noah. "Do you know what I do? I own 50 percent of this entire dealership. Our finances and roles in this dealership are the same. Stop acting like I am below you, because I am certainly not."

"I don't act like that!" Mark yells. Shut up! You're acting stupid."

"I'm not acting stupid," says Noah. "You think you're untouchable, and everybody is below you. Watch yourself. I've been watching this happen for a few days now, and I am sick of it."

This argument takes place at Mark's house. I sit upstairs and play video games. I hear everything, but act like I can't hear anything. I'm not present during a moment where I usually am present, that is, when Mark is angry like this. Any feeling of pity that I usually have now is absent. Emotions other than happiness have been turned off like a light switch. Noah walks quickly outside, slamming the door behind him.

I did well in getting Noah to contain his thoughts until they just erupted. The good news is that I know that the two men will reconcile soon, because their friendship is so close and because of the way I set this thing up. Noah is Mark's very close friend. However, Mark has been very angry lately and has said some things he didn't mean. Noah will return and apologize for his outburst, and Mark will apologize too. But for now, they do not know that, and, for me, this is the best part. I sit upstairs, and I can feel the vulnerability in the air. I can feel Mark's sadness and his powerlessness. I love it. Mark goes to his room, feeling impotent. He's waiting for me, helpless, I can feel it. He wants me to come to him and comfort him as I usually do. And usually I do feel pity, but now it is gone, unavailable. Instead, I sit here smiling. I feel so accomplished, so proud of my successful planning. But then something strange happens. I break my own rules.

I go downstairs to Mark. For once in my life, I'm not in control of myself. I feel obliged to explain. I speak all my evil thoughts aloud. I tell him that I believe I can manipulate large groups of people, the entire population. I tell him that I set up his fight with Noah, that I constructed this vulnerability he is feeling. I tell him he never will be as intelligent as I am. I tell him that he angered me and made me want to terrorize him, to handicap him.

"Why? Why are you having these thoughts, Zach?" asks Mark.

"You don't know what you did to me," I say. "You're blind. You can't see anything." I am no longer trying to prove a point; I'm just angry and hurt.

"What did I do? Is this because I yelled at you, Zach?" he asks.

"No! Shut up, Mark!" I yell, trembling. "Don't you remember what you said? You undermined me! You told me I was heartless! You told me I was never there for you, that I was self-consumed and selfish."

"Zach, just listen," he says. "I …"

I cut him off quickly. "Shut the hell up! You're the one who is heartless, not me! Do you know how long I sat under your heels, cleaning up after you, justifying your wrongs? I went against my own morals to support you. I never turned away! I wanted to sit upstairs and hear you break down. I wanted to feel it!" I'm shaking. I grab his can of soda and throw it at the wall. He sits on his bed, back upright. He is motionless, quiet. He isn't talking; he is just watching.

"I am not heartless," I continue. "I think about everybody, all the time. You're too stupid and oblivious to see it. You're too inconsequential to see anything. Don't ever try and tell me I'm heartless, when you know what I go through for you and for everybody around me. You know how much I love Sarah and Mia. I told you! If you'd ever listened, you would know. The sisters whom I barely see, whom I need. I don't have them! All I want to do is go to Santa Barbara and take them. I want to be with them. I want to be with you and the rest of the family, but you guys never see the good in me. You guys just talk shit about how horrible I am. But Sarah and Mia don't feel that way. They are the only family I have who do not see me as a sociopathic freak." For the first time in years, I'm crying, and I'm shaking too.

"Nobody knows what it is like to spend the whole flight back and forth from California, and all the airport time, and the next few days feeling an extremely painful amount of guilt," I tell him. "Dying inside, unable to breathe. I punch my chest hard constantly, to try and get my guilt and hurt to subside, but it's unavoidable. I keep feeling this guilt that I am not able to describe in words!" I lie on the ground, screaming, and crying. "I will make you regret anything bad you ever said to me," I continue. "I will make you regret your lack of appreciation! Watch me, because I'm powerful!"

As I yell out these words, my head on the ground, Mark grabs me and hugs me. I try and push him off. I don't want him to touch me. But he is hugging me so hard that I can't get him off me. It is odd that I cannot push him off, even though I am physically superior. I am now sobbing in his arms. I am the one who is never supposed to feel vulnerable. I am the one who always knows what is going on. I am the one who governs my thoughts! But now I am lying in someone's arms.

Mark hugs me tighter and says, "I know you love them more than any person has ever loved anything." Then we sit silently for a few minutes, while I try to dry the tears of agony from my eyes.

"I'm sorry, Zach," Mark says. I should have praised you and taught you that you are a great person. I should have let you know." And then he hugs me more tightly than I've ever been held and says something that changes my perspective on life itself. "Zach, this is what it feels like to be loved." When he says that, I choke, and I shake. I never have been loved before.

———◆◆—◆◆—◆◆———

A week and a half after that sentimental moment, I am livelier. I am giving this whole love thing a try. I try to love people, to be compassionate. I now know what it is like to be loved. I've felt it. I am now kinder to those around me. I am not as stubborn. But most of all, I do not exhibit the severe arrogance I projected in the past. Perhaps I no longer think about my gift, my remarkable intelligence, because I now know what it means to be human. I know how it feels to have regular human emotions, including pain—to feel anything other than anger and pride.

I talk, walk, and act differently. The change in my behavior should be obvious to any individual who knows me. Life needs another chance, so I walk around with an open mind. However, there one person who isn't seeing my contribution; as hard as I try, she cannot see it. Day and night, I think about human emotions and what my attitude to life should be. Still, she does not see it. The more I think about it, though, the more I realize that it is her loss, and I will not dwell in sorrow because of my mother's inability to see the new, golden me. Perhaps she can't see what surrounds her? That must be it. As she lies on her bed, watching movies and TV all day and all night, is she losing the ability to read other people, even her own son—who has stuck with her through the worst and the best of times. I am the son who acts like a sponge, sucking in all her depression because she is unable to contain it. *Snap back to your regular self, Zach!* She is your mother and only has love for you; it's just that depression gets to her.

My mom always asks me, "Do you know what it is like to have no self worth? To feel like you have nothing to live for?" No, I cannot say that I know how that feels—when one bleeds love for himself, that's the opposite of what he will ever feel.

I answer my mom by telling her, "Mom, to be completely honest. I am a narcissist. I only love and care for myself. I am never insecure about anything."

She responds, "That is a lie. Insecure is all that you are."

"You don't even know your own son," I say in a very aggressive tone.

"You think you are great, but that is just a cover up for your weak side, your fragile side, your insecure side." When she says things like that, I stop talking. I sit motionless and ponder about the truth in the words she utters. Is it even possible to cover up insecurity and self-hatred with an unmatched sense of self-love, as she says I do? The more I think about this, the stricter I am with myself. I need to control my thoughts more. I cannot keep thinking about what she says. But there is one thing she says that absolutely perplexes me: "You're scared to get hurt, so you stop caring about people. You know that if you get too close to people, they'll hurt you, so you run away from your emotions and try to convince yourself that you do not love. Zach, you are an emotion-fearing human."

The more I think about what she's said, the more fury pumps through my arteries. I don't fear love; I don't fear anything. I do fear one thing, and that is God. Nothing and no one other God scares me. What my mom is incapable of understanding is that I don't feel love, except for my family at certain times and for Albert. That is the only love that I have for anyone at all. Any sense of intimacy that is directed toward me disturbs me. I get agitated and confused when a girl tells me she loves me; I enter a realm of pure, raw arrogance. I feel the impurities in everybody around me and believe I am on a level that no one can understand. No one can top my intelligence.

CHAPTER 2

The news spread across the school on the first day. Nobody really knew him before his death, but now they all apparently do. All they knew then was that often hung out with me. All they care to know now is that he committed suicide.

The next day, the school staff hold a ceremony in his honor in the cafeteria. All students are required to attend this gathering. There are whispers everywhere, some laughter, and a lot of fake tears, as we all come together and sit on the cafeteria chairs. The principal stands up and says,

> Today, we are all gathered to remember a kind soul who is no longer with us. A young man who was kind to every person he ever encountered. Wyatt Kimmel took his life yesterday. It is hard for us to understand why he did this. But he was a very good young man, and we can never forget that. Instead of mourning his death, we should try to remember his life and his welcoming attitude toward everybody. Let us all pray that our demons never get to us the way that Wyatt's demons affected him. Rest in peace, Wyatt. Thank you, everybody. Now let's listen to a few words from some of the teachers and students who were close to Wyatt.

Fake tales are told, and people say that he was such a good kid. Teachers and office staff take advantage of this moment to give little speeches about bullying and their after-school therapy program. They tell the students that is it not embarrassing to be in therapy. Then the principal calls on me. "Zachariah would like to say a few words about Wyatt, so I expect everybody's full attention. Please stand up, Zachariah, and take the microphone."

I walk to the center of the cafeteria, pulling on the sleeve of my sweater with blue stripes, the same sweater I wore when I was last with Wyatt. I try and prepare myself for to say something, which now feels completely impossible. How can you be even slightly prepared for a moment like this? My chest hurts. Vanity and audience. Vanity and audience. How do those two correlate? How will my narcissism hold up against an audience of more than two thousand people giving their full attention to what I must say. Also, add my torn heart to the equation.

This an evaluation of my confidence level, an opportunity to show people that I am high and mighty. *Snap out of it, Zach!* That kid who used to hang out with me after school, who poured out his heart to me, is no longer alive. This isn't a time to think about vanity and my pride. Shame on me! No. There's a reason these thoughts keep coming at me: I haven't yet acknowledged the fact that this isn't a regular day. *Talk now. I must start speaking now.*

I stand tall, hold the mic tightly near my mouth, and say,

> I was sitting on a bench after school, on the fourth day, when I first met Wyatt. By the last month of school, we were very close. He used to tell me about his problems and about his pain, I cannot believe that he never told me anything as serious as this. I've been playing it in my mind all day, frantically trying to discover why he did this.

I get louder and more passionate. "I've been trying to understand why he took his own life. I loved Wyatt like a brother." I stop for a moment because my chest is pounding. My heart feels like it is going to pop right out. The pain has hit; I can feel my arteries pumping blood through every part of my body—my skull, forearms, biceps, feet. "Wyatt was a good person, and he would have become something great." Tears begin streaming down my face, and I cry softly. My chest feels like it is bulging. "I will always remember Wyatt and I hope you do too." I keep crying; I am no longer able to hide my tears. I sit down, and my friends pat me on the shoulder and give me heartfelt hugs. I feel supported; the people around me are diminishing my pain.

When I get home from school, I run to my room and lie in bed where I am ambushed by my own thoughts. Too much has happened all at once. I wish it were not the death of somebody that made me feel this way. All day, I thought about two things: Wyatt and my own vanity and obsessions. After the ceremony of remembrance for Wyatt, almost every student in the high school hugged me. They told me that things would be okay and that they would all remember him. Hundreds of people showed me love that day; it was the most fascinating thing I have ever seen.

> Wyatt, I beg of you, do not to turn this into an upside for me. Don't make me so plagued by my obsession that I am unable to feel the proper grief. Don't keep me locked in this cage of terror alone, where I can't feel grief without thinking about myself and my dysfunctional characteristics. Don't allow me to become polarized into narcissism and dread, I beg of you.

When I think about Wyatt, my heart shreds. That innocent kid sat next to me on the bench in the beginning of the school year and stayed by my side every day for eight months. He killed himself! He used to tell me who he wanted to be in life; he was always thinking about his aspirations. He had ambition. He had so much ambition. It was in the air he breathed; it even got into my senses. He wanted to be an author; he wanted to write fantasy stories, stories about his family's struggles, etc. And he was a damn good writer. He could have written an entire book about anything, even the placement of a pencil on a table. I recognized his creative sophistication.

Damn it! Damn the world around me! This potent mixture he stirred up in my bloodstream is agonizing. Why would he tell me about his aspirations and then kill himself? What a coward! *No, Zach, keep it together!* He wasn't a coward. Nobody knows what he went through. Whatever it was, he could not live with it. His death was infuriating and destructive, but he was a tortured soul. And I will have to learn to cope with that very simple explanation for why Wyatt killed himself: he was a tortured soul.

I loved him. I cared about him. But I can't understand why he killed himself. It hasn't even completely registered in my mind. He took his own life. I will never see him again; not even for one more minute will he be on this earth! Wyatt hung himself. He knew what he was doing; it was a conscious decision. I do not understand, but I can't dwell on it. It will only make my night worse.

Kinglike pride. Godlike fanaticism. It has all died; every ounce of my contentment with myself has gone. My vanity has perished. I have become an emotional cripple, lower than the lowest. My low self-worth is choking me. Nobody is here to help me get through this; nobody sees it. How can people be so blind? Family aid is scarce. Signs of affection are irregular. Yet they have the audacity to label *me* heartless. I will never forget this. I've suffered a great loss, and I still have the same uncaring family. Screw the blood between us; they are ill. They preach about moral conduct, respect, values, etc., but behind closed doors they are teaching the art of neglected emotions. Stress, depression, fazed—they're all understatements. I am a seriously ill person among the dead; almost lifeless, with very mild evidence of life in me.

This isn't normal. My friend committing suicide is not a regular, everyday activity. My friend wrapped a rope around his throat and hung himself from the ceiling. Every organ in his body was put to rest, forever! Now the scariest part in all of this is that I now am being choked, near the point of death. I am being choked by self hatred. Wyatt did not just kill himself, he killed much of me with him! I am only in tenth grade and already I am dead inside. My vanity is virtually nonexistent.

———◆◆◆◆———

It just keeps getting worse; my life is a living hell. And even though, unlike Wyatt, I am not one to flee from my problems, I can relate to him at this point. I can relate to the desire to just live as a blank. However part of the core of my religion is understanding that suicide is a ticket to the fires of hell.

Unhealthy living. I have been living like a recluse for the past three weeks. Never, not for one day in my life, have I ever thought that I would remotely reach depression. But here I am—unable to concentrate at school, or to stop thinking about Wyatt. I don't want to be around my friends. I see them all now as nuisances. I am tired of it all and hurt. I have been social throughout my life. I have had friends. But I have never been obeyed, surrounded, watched, and idolized like I was after Wyatt died. I felt like an icon or a celebrity. I realize now, in my depressed state, that I am not a narcissist. I am the opposite. In fact, I wish I were a narcissist. I'm not able to love myself or anybody else for that matter. I had this obsession to get recognition from others, because my so called "high self-esteem" was almost nonexistent. I needed approval and very much of it. I lacked confidence in who I was. I was proud of my ability to control minds, and I used those manipulative mind-controlling tendencies to control people. Now the one mind I should be able to control, my own, is governed by emotions of self-hatred. The day after Wyatt died, I cried in front of more than a thousand people. When I walked out of the cafeteria, hundreds of people followed me and offered their condolences; that was the worst day of my life, looking back at it now. My heart is locked in a chamber with its only roommate—dread.

Remember Wyatt's aspirations? Wyatt was going to be a writer; he was going to be one of the best storytellers of the modern era. As I lie on my king-size bed, which feels like it is too small for me, I realize something powerful. To continue his legacy, I want to at least try to do what Wyatt wanted to do. I want to try to write about all the pain I am going through and my absent love for humanity. I do love my family, mainly Sarah and Mia. However, I have this overwhelming hatred for humanity. The world is composed of selfish and self-consumed idiots.

I need to put these ideas into action now. I need to write now! I stand straight up from on my bed and walk over to the drawer. As I walk across the room, I see a tool that I have used to destroy myself and those around me. I look up at the thought wall—my perceptions, personified

I can't ignore that there are good thoughts on the thought wall. All my thoughts and ideas are recorded there, good, and bad. But right now, all I can see are the bad thoughts. Blinded by anger, I furiously tear down the past eight months of my life. I take out the supplier of hate for my childhood that lived on the thought wall, the manipulative traits—all recorded in times of stress. Down goes the good with the bad. I tear this project down. With every paper that I take down, I cry more and more tears of fury and frustration. The devil lives in this wall, which told me to hurt Mark, to cause emotional imbalance in Alexa, to hate my mother and my family, to control people's minds. It told me I wasn't earning enough respect, that I was underappreciated. That wall convinced me, really convinced me, that I was dangerous.

Once I've torn the thought wall to pieces and throw it away, I snatch a notebook from my drawer and grab a pencil from the top of the fish tank. I open the notebook, lay it flat on the table with my pencil in hand, and then start writing. I start something that will change the world.

<hr />

My tan arms glow in the sun. Being in Oklahoma City at noon on a day in early May is like being in the middle of the Sahara Desert. Luckily I am in the car; the air conditioning running, so the heat isn't as excessive. I am waiting on my older brother, Muaz, to leave the doctor's office. It is a long wait. He doesn't come to the doctor to treat an illness or get prescriptions. He comes to the doctor because he wants to make money. He is creative in only one category, and that is acquiring money. He expresses his inner businessman, talking the way they all do—describing fake life experiences, showing off. When he talks business, he starts off nice and properly introduces himself, offering a firm handshake and staring into the eyes of the person to whom he is speaking. He then tells highly exaggerated stories about how he built himself up from scratch, how he drives around in the finest of cars, intelligent and stupid business decisions he's heard about, and his ideas for creating business empires. His aim is to appear as successful as he can, in as realistic a manner as possible. This gives the impression that he is the hardest of workers, and it would be a tragedy to not work with him. Muaz talks to bigger people with money—physicians, established entrepreneurs, marketers, etc.—established people who can hold up their ends of the bargain and earn him money. I don't quite how he does the things he does. He claims that he owns land and can make up to $50,000 in a two - or three-month period. He is eighteen years old. Is what he says true or false? I wouldn't know, because he might be telling me the same things he tells to everyone else. All I do know is that he does have clients, because I drive him places. Right now, we are at one of the top five wealthiest vascular surgeons in the whole state of Oklahoma.

Money drives Muaz, which is honestly so sad. But that is just my opinion. Still, I could give a hundred thousand reasons why accomplishing what you love is more significant than earning of money as an end. I could counter every argument anyone would make about why money is more fulfilling than success in something that truly defines someone, success in something someone truly loves.

This wait in the car is taking too long. I have been sitting in this parking lot under this oak tree for about two hours. Free time is all I have right now; my phone's battery is very low. I cannot use my phone for any reason other than emergency. But my notebook and pencils are in the glove compartment. They are among my most valuable things. I won't forget, however, what is most valued by me—I can say it a hundred times over—my two little sisters, Mia and Sarah, my pearls.

This cruel world has been on my mind lately, so I need to free my thoughts, to record them through poetry. I start by writing anything that comes to mind, just a few lines of poetry to burn time quickly.

> Psychotic is the woman who deems her man noble;
> Conceited is the man who takes vocal ownership of
> his woman.
> Detoxified is the heart that goes through break.
> Worthless is the fortune that incriminates.
> Intelligent is the creative.
> Evil is the man who turns a blind eye toward wrong.
> Subjective judgments become our only judgments,
> vicious cycles of teaching morals as hypocrites.
> Forgotten is the ability of self-reliance.
> Dependency is the dominant igniter of all evil stories.
> Mixed in too often with good is evil.
> Fearing it all are the type of men who seldom
> encounter the real world; instead, they hibernate
> like the winter bear.

All kind speech is a hoax.

Absent is the heart of the man who sees it all.

All stories improperly depict real life, causing false belief in the structure of life, false belief that many call imagination.

Exaggeration is the core of conversation.

Tormented are the ones who claim to be happy.

Beasts living among us control us; are they us?

Or are they invisible beasts that play with our lives and livelihood?

Craving satisfaction, man alters his state.

Consciousness runs out on us, fades into the darkness, returning only when it desires to.

Life is pottery, orbiting the fingers of men until the idea of perfection is successfully constructed.

These deep thoughts, jumping in my head, need to be written down. There are more of them. There are too many. I am hiding from something. I am hiding from Wyatt; I haven't talked to him since he died. There is only one way I can to talk to him—through my writing.

This ode is for you, Wyatt. You need to know what I am going through.

To Wyatt Kimmel,

Remember when you once told me that I was deaf, and I yelled at you harshly? I told you that I see and hear everything. I told you that I can observe on a level few humans are capable of, and that my memory is excellent. I want you to know that I hate that I said that. I manipulated you into seeing me as some type of supernatural human being, and that was wrong. However, there was element of truth in what I said. The truth is that I do observe and remember unlike regular human beings. I add thoughts together in the fastest and most successful ways. I drift into my thoughts easily, because I go through so many thoughts quickly. However, the mind of relevance that I have, the detailed mind that reaches the significant part in seconds is the reason for my illness. I am writing this to tell you that it is your fault I am ill, emotionally, and mentally. The mind that I once hailed as great, amazing, and the source of happiness is the reason for my distress and grief. I think intensely, and anytime I try to think about anything in the damn world except you, I cannot. My thoughts always somehow return to thoughts of dread, thoughts of you. I hate you Wyatt. You killed something deep inside of me, and every day I grow colder than the day prior. No, I don't hate you, Wyatt. I love you; you were a good person. I should be honest with you, however. I don't know if I am depressed right now because *you* died or because of death itself. But I do know you meant a lot to me while you were alive. You have been making me think a lot about death lately. You have reminded me that man is mortal not everlasting. You have reminded me that although I am not the most religious person, there is a greater power above us. I have been searching and reading the Quran lately, and there is one verse that I keep returning to: "Every soul shall taste death." I must tell you: I hate that you killed yourself. I don't know if it was cowardice; if this world treated you so harshly, you could not live in it; or if some demon was living in your consciousness. I keep trying to understand everything that happened, but I find myself unable to understand why. Why did you do it?

Your mom invited me to your house the other day. Your sister, Morgan, and your dad were there too. Your mom brought out some tea for all of us to sip on while we were sitting at the table. We talked about academics and your dad's car business. Nobody at the table brought up your name for a good fifteen minutes, until I ignorantly asked about the skateboard leaning against the wall in the living room.

"Mrs. Kimmel, that skateboard is really nice. Is it Morgan's?" I asked.

"Zach." She chuckled softly. "That skateboard was Wyatt's. He loved riding it around the neighborhood. He used to go all the way to the corner store. He loved being alone with his skateboard and his thoughts."

I hate that my curiosity led me to ask about the skateboard. I could see your mom tear up a little. But what did I think? Did I think I would spend two entire hours at your house and not bring up your name once? That is not possible; bringing you up was inevitable.

Your dad started talking about the skateboard, and the more we talked about you, the more our hearts broke.

"One time he was riding the skateboard on the block in front of the house," your dad said, "and I was watching him through the window. He fell on his arm, and his whole arm had a scrape, about four inches long and two inches wide. He did not come inside and ask for help. He was so independent. He went to the nearest drug store, bought some supplies, and took care of his arm all by himself. He put alcohol all over and wrapped his arm all over. When he came home, he had everything concealed under his sleeve, and he never talked about it. He was twelve years old."

After your dad talked about how independent you were, something occurred to me. Your independent personality is why I was sitting there at his family's table, talking about you. You killed yourself because demons haunted you. You were too weak to be able to live with yourself, because you weren't able to voice your anguish or pain. Something else occurred to me as well. I might become Wyatt if I stay on my destructive path.

I am the blessed version of you, Wyatt. I am the person who had the luxury of believing I was a narcissistic sociopath and nobody could harm me because of my intellectual abilities. I am the one with a strong consciousness and the more aware self. I am the one who somehow knew how to expel my anger by manipulating systems and devising plans. All the pain I went through was a gift in disguise. It was such a gift that I am not the one in a grave today, waiting for you to write an ode to me.

Thank you for the lesson you've taught me, childhood. I always knew there was a greater good in you. And thank you, Wyatt, for what you taught me about death. I love you for that.

Sincerely,
Zach

I put the pencil down, grab a napkin, and wipe away the sweat and tears. I grab one of the cold-water bottles in the back of the car and gulp up the water. My chest is breaking; I can't take this anymore.

My chest hurts so much. The pain is not only emotional, but physical. It's excruciating. I can't hold it in anymore. I feel dizzy, weak; I can't move. Paralysis affects my entire body. I am dead inside, dead outside. What happened? I am unable, to process thoughts or move. My eyes shut down uncontrollably. It's time to sleep.

———•—◆◆◆◆—•———

They know the story, but they don't know the full story. They don't know that it isn't because of the heat. I hate this. Lately, I have been loathing my very creation.

They know little about anything. Everybody stays ignorant about my well-being while I suffer inside. I am hospitalized; people come in. All they know is that I was sitting in the car, my body went through some type of shock, and I passed out. The truth is, I was emotionally broken. I fell apart. My body went through temporary paralysis. It seems like no big deal to them. They just give me the regular "I hope you are doing better" during the three days I am in the hospital. But I talked to a human being who no longer exists. That was Wyatt's way of responding to me, or maybe that was God's way of warding me off. Whatever it was, I got the message. I won't get close to anything like that again.

Everything since Wyatt's death has been a blur. The core of the issue is still something I have not been able to see, which is ironic because I have always had this supernatural ability to understand things quickly. However, when I look through my writings, I see several things: guilt, vulnerability, gloominess, anger, melancholy, happiness, relief, jealousy, and so many dark emotions. Emotions rise from the depths of my soul. I can't live like this anymore. So I decide to flip a switch, to change it all. I am motivated by experience in the mind and heart of the low.

I will continue to write like a man locked up in a chamber with nothing but a notebook and a pen. I will write until I can't write. I realize that writing is my escape from it all, from the trapped outcast that I am. My writing represents a change in life for many people; there is no other reason I was put here other than to reflect the way I see the earth, the perspective of Zach Smith, a human being who would need more than two hundred adjectives to describe his view of this world. The second thing I have decided to do in my new life is study like a lonely freak, to commit all my time to studying and writing. I realize that being social no longer holds any value to me; I don't need it, because I have had my fair share of it. I have gone through the phases of "controlling my audience's minds." I've had my fair share of friends and hanging out and messing around with girls—occasionally trying to embarrass them or lower their self-esteem. (I was ruthless.) I've had it all socially; now it is time to flip the page and to start the tale of the boy who gave everything up because he wanted to flourish academically. This is page 1 of my new story.

My notebook, my pencils and pens, my laptop, and my bag are the sole reasons for my newfound happiness. I have sudden bursts of energy, when I just want to pour my thoughts into a reservoir of writing like a broken fire hydrant. I will allow that reservoir to mass-produce works until it becomes a source of mimicry to the human heart. I want my writing to be so well polished so that I will lead men and women in a single-file line and tell them that there is much more to the world than what the naked eye sees and the naked heart feels. I will present the idea as a philosophical point of view, challenging the intellect of mankind.

People are dependent, which causes them to chase the foolish things. Everything may be tried, but until that need is satisfied, well, there is no way of escaping internal misery. People try to satisfy the need for dependence by using other people. That is the most insolent crime a person can commit—to get so close to someone that he or she becomes the only reason to get up in the morning, to even want to breathe. And that continues until their dependence on each other crashes into a wall and dies out. When one depends on something selfish like a human being and devotes his life to that person, melancholy surrounds their lives. Then comes the self loathing that hits them so badly that any defense mechanism they ever had becomes nonexistent and anything that desires to enter their hearts can enter with unbelievable ease. That is the reason I'm always so angry at the girls who told me they loved me; they infuriated me. If they knew the danger of their "love," they would run away from it. The heart is the evilest thing ever created, but ... *Zach! Stop getting distracted.*

The point is that I am trying to feed my need for dependence by finding something that will not break my heart. I am satisfying that need with hard work, more specifically, hours of writing and my schoolwork. Writings resurrects me. I have found happiness living as a recluse, secluding myself from the public, appearing only when truly needed or when I feel the desire to thrive. I love you, dear writing. This is for you. I take my notebook and brand new purple mechanical pencil out of my khaki bag and enter my realm of happiness. I begin.

> To writing,
>
> You have eclipsed everything I have ever truly loved, kindled the dark paths that I inevitably will walk upon. With guidance from you, I will be successful in all that I do. I will repel the evil in the souls around me and protect the souls of those I love. I am vulnerable without you, complete with you. I will carry on your legacy, with everlasting pride. Your nurturing causes me to love you more than love itself. I am becoming dependent on you.
>
> Before we pursue any journeys, however, I have a confession to make from the depths of my heart. I only tell you this because I am required to pay homage to you. I have more trust in you than I have in anything else.

For that very reason, I must clarify that I am a guilty human being, but I feel guilty about wrongs I did not commit. My mind is convinced of my innocence in the crimes against humanity, but I cannot convince my heart that I am innocent. Wholeheartedly, I feel as though I hurt the ones I love. The guilt tortures me in every waking moment; it tortures me in my sleep. There is no escape from the guilt, so I have no choice but to dwell in it. The pain of guilt chest is like the pain of twenty bricks stacked on my chest. This guilt has broken me and left me vulnerable beyond measure.

Oh, dear writing, the origin of the guilt starts with my two little sisters. They are halfway across the country. I am unable to live with that reality, so I mourn. I feel powerless, and I hate my reflection. Looking in the mirror is an excruciating reminder of the man who terrorized me. I am unable to forgive myself, so there are nights when I scream as though I am a demonic teacher attempting to teach a simple concept to stupid children. No matter how much I scream, my heart will not comprehend that I am not the source of this wrongdoing, that I am merely a victim. I can never escape this guilt.

The second reason for my guilt is the life of Wyatt. How did I walk next to a boy who was dying inside without even the faintest hint of it? I ask myself all day if I even somewhat understood the troubles he went through; the same answer comes to mind every time in the form of a question. How can I feel even an ounce of the hundreds of pounds of pain that boy suffered? That teenage boy was so completely and utterly torn apart by the deepest gashes of life that he took the unspeakable road—the suicidal road, the rode for the those who self-loathe beyond human capacity. How can I have walked with that tortured soul and not see even a drop of his blood? The guilt presents itself, because it knows that I was too consumed by my thoughts about my extraordinary capabilities to see the walking dead next to me. Sadder than all of this, it is not love for Wyatt that makes me dread my very existence; it is the conceptual difficulty of walking around as the highest exalted to such a low level that every breath taken is a question of my desire to live.

There is one final truth I would like to confess to you, dear writing. Subdued my thoughts of social competence have been the thoughts of escape through difficult amounts of work. I jot this down because I am too cowardly to ever think or say it aloud. The whole meaning behind my new change is not only because I desire flourishing academic success; it is also because of the depression of my spirits, my melancholy. If there were documented levels of how much self-worth is contained within a human being, one could see that my love and self-worth went from the highest to a disturbingly low level, so that the very few bits of it left are to be directed unto myself. I realize that I am incapable of loving anybody else due to my very low love capacity. Attempting to hide from this, I repeatedly tell myself that this is because I desire academic success and have a strong desire to write. With every thought or word, I utter about the reasoning behind this new life, there is the heart that recognizes that they're all lies.

Oh, dear writing, I dearly love you, and I have chosen to share with you invisible and dark thoughts and feelings. I express these thoughts because I see a great future in pursuing you, dear writing. So, I will continue to write, through both the darkest times and the happiest times, such as when my greatest worries were to determine what was true in my childhood's teachings. This is the start of a new story and an everlasting love for you, oh dear writing.

CHAPTER 3

I sit in this room; just me, all alone. Occasionally, people come in to say hello, ask how I am doing. I answer by saying I'm good, just working on something; then they walk out. My room is probably the most secluded of the five bedrooms in this house. I have a nice and quite space for myself; there is a brown desk in the right corner near the window, a bed between the desk and a seventy-five-gallon fish tank. Behind me, is my recliner and to the right, a TV on a table. There was a time almost four years ago, when I was in my freshman year of high school, that I would spend hours on end playing video games with friends or watching TV. Life was great in that time of simplicity. I felt the Oklahoma breeze; I always had that nice gym sweat. Life was good then. Now, as I sit at my desk on my black leather chair, the highlight of my day is taking out my phone and looking through pictures of my friends—people I no longer see or talk to.

Although I do miss those earlier, good times, I am appreciative of my brown desk and secluded bedroom. This desk has been my good friend for two years. The desk and I have great chemistry; I have cried on it, sweated on it, smiled on it, written on it, screamed at it, hit it, hugged it, and talked to it. This desk is my kindest caretaker; it takes care of me. When I don't want to sit behind it and work, it contacts my conscience, which nags at me until I sit back down behind the desk.

This desk is the biggest source of my happiness, because my best writing happens here. I have been writing like a possessed soul every since the suicide. I went through my sophomore year and my junior year with hard-earned grades. I worked harder than any person I have ever known, and still I do. Now, in my last few months of high school, time is a little more negotiable. I prepare myself for college and do some work, but overall, my hard and tiring high school years are ending. If only everybody else knew what I have written, and the value my writings hold. I compile millions of letters to become more than just words; they are mankind's missing link. If my books are ever published, the world would be a different place.

This is not only because I believe in my literary abilities; it is because my thoughts do not occur in the regular human mind. I can reach into a part of the heart and brain that the rest of the world is not able to find. I write in stories; there are no autobiographical elements to the writing. These are stories of other men and women, people I stress out because I expose their souls and powerful secrets. These books one day will be open, and the readers will see books that break the filter of the mind—intellectually.

I'm not actually completely alone in this room. It may sound funny, but some supernatural activity goes on in this room. I wake up at different times during the night and sit up straight; sometimes, I see something walk out of the room quickly. I don't hear anything; there are no traces of its presence. But I do see them occasionally. And I feel them; there are beasts living with me. I know that people will argue they are just figments of my imagination, and they could be correct, but I do feel spirits around me—walking near me, influencing my thoughts and feelings. When I write, I sometimes have an overwhelming sense of anger, very odd moments of deep anger. I do not get angry easily. I get gloomy, sad, guilty, hurt, excited, maybe agitated, but I never get the kind of anger that rises when I sit alone in my room. During these extreme moments of anger, I get these urges to tear into somebody's flesh. I want to slit their throats; I want to terrorize people.

My angry writing, my regular writing, is poetry about hatred of life—a description of how to terrorize mankind in the most eloquent manner. My theories are intended, in many ways, to show the injustice in this world. I know there are spirits in my room, because when during those painfully angry moments, times, I can feel my blood pounding, as if I am having a seizure. These spirits exist and, sadly, they motivate me. The beasts are influencing me.

━━━◆◆◆◆━━━

I went through times of war and negligence during which I repelled every person who tried to talk to me. It is weird to watch someone go from friendly and social—having all the friends he could ever want—to walking around with his head down, alone in his own zone, not communicating with anybody. That was me. That is still me. It is my only way of appeasing the guilt. I frown at myself when I think about those times. I left everybody. I became a different kind of human. Many people ask why; many do. I've never answered them completely, even after two years. I do not blame them for their curiosity. After all, I turned into an antisocial outcast, which doesn't happen to popular kids.

I decided to live my new life, but I still talk to a few people, particularly Albert. I can never walk away from Albert, in good or bad times. I can never keep him out of my life. He is the best friend I've ever had. We call each other regularly about basketball and the NBA. We both like the same team, the Houston Rockets. We follow their every play like hawks; the team entertains us. Watching the Rockets is one reason I maintain my sanity. Albert is another. There are things I regret about my friendship with Albert. Two years ago, I was depressed because of Wyatt; for the first two weeks, Albert tried frantically to reach out to me, but I ignored him. I neglected our friendship. Wyatt's death did not excuse that. Albert has been nothing but a brother to me, and it was wrong to neglect our friendship, even during hard times.

Albert was always a freak. He bit his nails and was always nervous. One could sense Albert's nervousness from a mile away. Albert was the needy one, the one who depended on me for guidance. I wish we could go back to those days, but our friendship has changed. I am now the one who wants to be around him. He taught me about loyalty, but I can sense his disloyalty.

I often ask what happened: "Why are you no longer as welcoming as you were in the past?"

I get the same answer every time: "I am. I've just been busy, dude. I still am."

Maybe he is as busy as he says he is. Whatever the reason, I do not see him as often as I used to. I've gone from seeing him at least once a week to seeing him once every two to three months. It may truly be my fault; I gave up on so much good. I know deep down inside that he does not want to be around someone like me, the person I have become—depressed, self-consumed, plagued. He will never say it, but I know he loathes the person I have become.

I ask myself, Did I really have a reason to run away, to conceal my fear for life in my writing and seclude myself? Was it justifiable? If I could go back, would I change what I did? These questions go on through my head often; these questions are what I have become. My answers to these questions varies depending on my very mood. When the spirits haunt and anger me, I answer these questions by blaming this unfair world, by questioning God and his so-called "mercy." When I get in my quiet and thoughtful moods, my answers are gloomy. I blame myself for everything. I blame myself for Wyatt's death, for Sarah and Mia being far away. I blame myself for mourning, for being cowardly. Then I enter this realm of writing, where I have no reason to blame myself. Instead, I blame life. I tell stories about other people who have gone through the same thing. I make in my characters unstable, which gives me the greatest opportunity to question the nose that allows me to smell, the mouth that allows me to breathe and eat, the legs that allow me to walk. I question the death of a fish in my tank or the fall of a pencil from my desk. This world is a large, abstract mixture of illusions. And I too have become too capable sometimes, in a literary sense.

—————◆◆◆◆◆◆————

Medicine can nullify emotional and psychological pain. Many things can be done about pain, but there is not much one can do about guilt. To this day, as an eighteen-year-old, as a man, I mourn over Mia and Sarah. Guilt comes in ugly, unpredictable ways, but never like this. I never tell my sisters about it, about the guilt. I never show them my weak side; it is better for them to live in contentment. I hold in tears when I video chat with them, call them, or travel to see them. These two girls are my pearls, and I pray there comes a day when we can all live with each other—a day when I don't have to deal with my insane mother, and neither do they. All I want for my pearls, Sarah, and Mia, is peace.

Sometimes I grab a piece of paper and dedicate some words to them. I never show those words to them, however, because of the emptiness it may bring to either them or me. I do write them down and lock them in the drawers of my desk. This is an example of something I wrote about four months ago:

Dear Sarah and Mia,

Do you know that I sing to you, about you? I swear, this isn't a joke. There are nights when I write lyrics about your beautiful green eyes, Sarah, and how they kindle my soul. Your green eyes are the most beautiful aspect of life. And your beautiful smile, Mia, gives me motivation to live. Sarah and Mia, if only you could understand, there are no hearts as kind as yours. There is no night as beautiful as the nights when I think about you. There is no beauty as divine as yours. I love you two very much.

Sometimes things try to snatch what we have; did you know that? Seriously, they do; they bring their big scissors and try to cut that thread in our hearts. Sarah and Mia, our hearts weave themselves back together. Let somebody cut the strings; who cares? Our hearts will always find a way to bring them back together. I shall cease to exist without your love. The aperture that God so elegantly crafted keeps me humble, like a wise old man.

Through my happiest and saddest times, dear Mia and dear Sarah, you are the loves of my life. I love no one else the way I love you two. Tears go through my heart when I see you cry. I will always be your big brother, through the snow and the rain, through the hot and the cold, through the smiles and the cries, through the whispers and the screams, through the nights and the days, through the evil and the good. I will always watch you with vigilance. You are the two greatest beings who walk this earth. Again, I love you two, my pearls, very much.

Fondly,
Zach

I have written much deeper words for Sarah and Mia; to unleash these words, however, would traumatize my emotions. One day, I will take all these notes and read them, on the days I doubt my desire to live. No doubt that day will come soon.

I swear, no matter what I do, no matter how much I try to fix what is so clearly broken, she will never apprehend my will to live happily with her. My mother is a strong reason I feel so low. For one second, I wish she could look up and see that I am trying to fix our relationship. I wish so that she could feel my pain even slightly. People ask why I have such anger flowing through my veins; much of it is because I am unappreciated. I've spilled so much blood, sweat, and tears, but she cannot see that.

Before I bash my mother, before I go to my brown desk and feed my hunger with the food of literature, before I use my writing to impeach every move she makes, I think about some words a wise man once told me. He was a man in the army who I met in the locker room at my gym. We were sitting on the benches, watching the Oklahoma Thunder play the Denver Nuggets. We conversed about our lives. I made a comment that he took to the heart. I said, "I would go into the army if my mom was not so scared for no reason. She definitely won't let me go."

He looked at me, smiled, and said, "Young men like you should try to understand the love a mother has for her kids, no matter what."

"I know she probably does love me very much," I said, "but she neglects me and my brother. She ..."

He cut me off. "First of all, your mother loves you more than life. She cares about you. All mothers do. Find the reason for her negligence. It could be because she is very stressed out. Second of all, never say bad things about your mom to anybody, especially somebody you do not know. Do you understand me?" I nodded my head.

"I used to think just like you," he said. "I wanted to flee from my mother. I never wanted to be around her. Look where I am now, I fight for my life. I have no opportunities for love, because I do not have any time. All I want to do now is tell her I love her, every minute of the day.

I tell her sorry, but it never feels like enough. I love her so much, and I regret the ill feelings I had for her I had when I was younger and stupid."

The passion in his words was genuine. I'll never forget what he said, even though I still get angry with my mom. His words remind me how many changes I need to undergo. I need to fix this—not tomorrow or anytime later. I need to fix this now. My mother and I need to start on a new page.

I try get up from my recliner, but my long legs make it hard. However, I have to do this, so I make one push to get up. I put my phone down on the recliner and walk downstairs. She gave all of us this house; although she does very little work now, there were times when she did do very much. Those times of hard work are the reason we live in this nice house and have this lifestyle. I get downstairs, my bare feet on the cold tile, and walk into her room. She is watching a movie on her tablet.

"Mama?" I say. She pauses the video and looks up at me.

"Yes, Zach," she says, in Arabic.

"I have been thinking a lot about you a lot," I say, "about our childhood, about now. I have so many good thoughts."

She says, "Is this …"

I cut her off, politely. I don't want her to disturb my train of thought. "I miss you, and I love you. Staying alone in my room makes me feel sick sometimes."

"I love you too, Zach. Give me a hug love," she says in half Arabic, half English. I get on her bed and hug her; she hugs me back tightly.

"I missed you so much, Zach," she says.

"I missed you too, Mama. I am sorry."

"No, Zach, I am sorry. You shouldn't be," she says, tearing up as she talks. Wait, why is she sorry? I am her son. I should be sorry for completely ignoring her.

"Mama, why are you sorry? I should be sorry, not you."

"No, Zach," she says, with tears going down her chubby face. "I should have given you more attention. That is why you are so distant."

"What do you mean? You …" She cuts me off the second I start talking.

"No, listen. Throughout your life, I cared more about looking after your brother. I forgot about you. I analyzed everything around you, but you. I understand that you are older now. However, I know it still bothers you, even if you don't know it. I am sorry, Zach, and I hope you can forgive me one day."

"I forgive you, Mama. It doesn't bother me. I am very tired though, so I am going to go to sleep."

"Goodnight," she says in Arabic.

"Goodnight," I reply, in Arabic.

I close the door behind me. Instead of taking a left and going up the stairs, I take a right and go sit in the living room. It is 1:00 a.m. on a school night. I should be sleeping, but I lie down on the big, brown, cushioned leather couch. I look up at the ceiling, my so very high ceiling; twenty-five feet of open space. This ceiling is like my mind, with more empty than occupied space. Every time I think I understand my mind, myself, I am hit with life. I learn that I am ignorant. This ceiling is all open space, never filled, like my mind; on second thought, like my emotions. I was neglected, as my mother said. Negligence causes independence, especially when a parent neglects a child. One question comes to mind: what is independence?

Is independence the ability to live freely with your thoughts without depending on another for emotional and spiritual guidance? Or is independence a big hoax that conceals so many important, basic, and positive human emotions, like love and happiness, or even the negative emotions, like hatred, fear, anger. It may be that independence is misinterpreted, even by those who believe themselves to be independent.

Life comes at costs; everything good has a cost. At times, paying the cost may be worse than avoiding the problem in the beginning.

The fire burns me badly, so I jump into the water. The water completely kills the fire, successfully ridding my body of any thermal energy. But again, everything has a cost. Happiness comes at a cost. Running away from one's problems has a cost. The love of this world has a cost; the hate of this world has a cost. Jumping into the water to stop the fire from burning me puts my lungs into an endangered position. I cannot swim; I am unable to breathe. In this scenario, I may have paid with my life to stop the fire from burning me.

I am among the neglected, among the abandoned. So said my mother and caretaker. My body lacks love and emotional leadership—two of the most basic human characteristics. My question to you, oh government of emotions: is my concealment of emotions the reason for my extraordinary ability to adjust? My emotions are so portable, I can adjust to a new situation with unbelievable ease. Or is that ability to adjust due to my intelligence? Has my intelligence given me such a profound understanding that I am able to reach the core of a problem and adjust with ease?

What if I took the three gallons of juice in my fridge and all juice that

I have ever had and replaced it with water? I would be able to live, but the question is how well?

While I am wrapped up in my thoughts, not even attempting to control them, an idea appears. An idea for a poem; first, little bits, and then more and more as I jog up the stairs. I grab my pencil and notebook and write:

"Following My Conscience"

By Zach Smith

The sun hides
In the ocean tides.
Throughout the night,
It sleeps in a deserted area until life resumes in the
morning and calls upon its light.
It is never right to fight,
But what if the only things you ever loved were taken
from your sight?
So now since it is justifiable,
And anything you do, you are not left liable,
Will you fight?
It feels so right,
So you prepare to fight,
But the stealer of your hopes and dreams is out of
reach.
He is over at the beach,
where the sun lays down to sleep.
He wants to keep everything that was taken from you.
Again, you find him hiding.
Not at all abiding
with what it is that you want back from him.
So now is it okay to fight?
It feels so right,

So with all your might
You gather yourself, because once you grab his throat
you will squeeze it as tight
As you can.
But oh man,
he nears and nears
toward you, until he just disappears.
All your biggest fears
were left in you, while the good in you was taken.
Taken to be forsaken?
Or does he hide it with him giving you the urge to
want to fight?
Would it then be right to fight?
When he hides it, where does he take it?
You must know in order to grow.
So map him you will,
and trap him you will.
So after trapping him with your words,
making them sound like the beautiful sounds of birds,
you may let him free.
So you could see
where he takes you. Think of him as the walking key,
a key to take back the good, so that I may be me.
So as you follow him from behind,
controlling his mind
with all these kind
and glorifying words
that sound like the beautiful sounds of birds,
he leads you into the water
You feel like you want to slaughter
him. But is it then right to fight?
Or shall you follow him as it approaches night?
So I continue to follow, follow him into the water,
my blood starts to get hotter,
but I continue to walk toward the water.

Now I walk into and through the water.
Oh man, this man has showed me an ability.
An ability to walk through the sea.
If only I opened my eye to see;
then maybe I would not have seen it right to fight.
So through the water, we walk
every move he makes I mock.
I mock as I walk out of respect;
wanting to dissect
his mind
and find
in him the good.
So much it is that I wish I could.
As I follow him more I see
him as a key
entire his empire, behind the beach.
Who knew that somebody like him could teach
me, eliminating my desire to impeach?
Now that I see him as one to teach, is it then right
to fight?
To grab hold of his neck tight.
Or is that unjust?
So unjust that a gust
of wind must
show me the true meaning of unjust.
In his empire,
we go up higher and higher;

as we get much higher, he turns around, wearing
clearly his best attire
and says that very much he does admire
me. How did he know I was behind him?
"You are as close to me as my limb," he replies.
"Yes, I can read your mind," he sighs.
Right now, he just defies

my concealment ability. "Oh and Zach, my name is conscience,
I am basically like your audience!"
Is it now right to fight?
If I did try to fight, the fight would be internal
Like writing in a hidden journal.
Now that I know I have a conscience, is it still me
that I want to be?
Or has my conscience
already left me out of options?
Was this war over before it started, or has it just begun?
Behind the water, where the sun
hides when it wants to run
And if there is to be war, will it ever end?
Will it ever end before I have to lend myself?
And see my love for everything descend
to such a low that inside I will know it has vanished?
And by then the good in me would have been banished.

———————

God created a very troubled type of human, a person we sometimes call a creative genius. But this type of human is a more special than a creative genius, a type for whom there aren't words to describe. These people are so creative, it seems like a punishment. They walk around staring at everything up and down, analyzing structures, thinking rapidly, focusing on twenty different things because it is impossible for them to limit their minds to one thing. These people smile through their pain and laugh through their anger. This is not because they are joyful people, but because they can think angry thoughts, happy thoughts, sad thoughts, and so many other thoughts the same time, because they control their own minds. These people curve their boundaries to suit their own liking. They are highly intelligent and operate at a different level than the rest of mankind. But where does the pain and punishment come in?

The punishment comes when they exceed their ability to contain their thoughts. When this happens, they are locked in cages with their thoughts. No man can wish a worse punishment upon somebody; no mindset is worse than living trapped in your thoughts. These are the crash and tumbles that happen to them. At this point, they fear their thoughts, because they make their locked chambers denser and denser. A man trapped within his thoughts is tortured at every point in his life.

And when these people grieve, nothing can be worse. The way their minds add thoughts together quickly, keeping thoughts relative to each other, makes them much more dangerous to themselves. Can you imagine being unable to escape from your negative emotions?

There are the lucky ones, however. They have found an ability to release some of their thoughts, which gives them a temporary break from their locked chambers. They include writers, poets, musicians, and writers. But some of these people haven't had the lucky guidance that others have. Some of them become trapped for so long that they cannot contain it; they have had terrible lives. Empathy, guilt, love, and remorse disappear and release a serial killer, someone unkind, who hates life and humankind, or a sociopathic fraudster, a person who mercilessly agonizes others.

As wrong as it sounds, I sympathize with these horrible people. Can you imagine, for just one second, not being able to forget something? Suppose you were haunted by everything that was ever told to you, everything that you ever felt. How could you not strike pain into people's lives? How could you not want to inflict pain on the cause of your suffering? Fortunate are the ones who find a cure for the pain that results from internalizing everything. Unfortunate are the ones who have been hurt badly and, needing to escape their thoughts and emotions, they stalk and give pain to others.

Lately, I have realized the most unusual and exotic thing in my life. I never believed that I would ever appreciate my childhood, because of its docility, but I do now. I should thank God for the subtle life I was given, even though it has never seemed like it. I can't be angry with my past, when I am self-reliant because of what happened in the past. I didn't have a terrible past. I never had a past that was as foul as the evil humans' past. Thank God, I did not have it worse. If my life had been worse, I would have tried to hurt the people I know.

Thoughts. My life is consumed by them. While I sit here and try to understand the psychology of good and evil, my legs grow numb. They fall asleep on me sometimes, when I sit down for too long, like when I write. It is unfortunate that it happens, but I don't know what I can do about it. Well maybe, I should jog and exercise.

I get up from the kitchen table and walk toward the door. With one leg still asleep, it feels like I am dragging it behind me and like there are bubbles popping in my leg. I open the front door, and start jogging slowly, despite the pain and numbness in my leg.

I run faster as the numb feeling goes away; soon, I am jogging at a pretty quick speed. I feel the wind blowing in my face, the wind of a hot Sunday in Oklahoma City. After a few minutes, I stop to take a breath. I am panting pretty hard, trying to get some oxygen in my system. Something or someone is watching me; I feel it. I know I sound like a wild animal right now, but I just feel invaded. Is it normal to suddenly get these feelings of suspicion? Maybe I have fulfilled some kind of predetermined prophecy. Maybe I am the chosen one. *No, stop it, these odd thoughts need to stop. Zach, you're becoming very peculiar; it is as if the silence took your sanity from you.* Nobody is watching me; it is time to return to my regular self. This is all just excitement caused by thoughts about my writing. Lost in thought, I forget to acknowledge that I am nothing. I am a needle thrown somewhere in the desert; that is what my accomplishments add up to. One day, maybe, I will go on a journey one day, but I don't know the type of transportation or the location.

I jog to the neighborhood pond, which is filled with nice bass and catfish. It is the most spectacular scene. I sit on the bench near the water. Some ducks watch me; they're probably expecting me to throw some bread at them. They watch me closely as I look at the view. I do have the potential to give them food; that is true. I am a human with bread at home; it may not be on me, but I do have some.

I don't want to go get bread, because I am too busy watching the ducks. It is like they are a message for me, in the midst of my thoughts about being watched because of my potential. These large ducks— with bright red crests around their eyes and white, red, black, and green feathers—are watching me for just that reason: my potential. It could be coincidence that these ducks are here by my side at the lake. Or perhaps this was all predetermined.

Nothing is as simple as it looks or seems; there is a reason and philosophy behind everything. From the placement of a pencil to the death of a person, there must be reason for it all. Whenever I feel like I know it all, I get slapped in the face with the idea that knowledge is plentiful. Maybe knowledge isn't the beginning of understanding; maybe understanding begins with the examination of philosophy.

I believe I have struck gold here at this lake. From this day forward, I will be driven by philosophy and reflection rather than look at the world as it is. There is a supernatural force, I know it—and not only because of the ducks and the pond. I knew it before. I just needed a slap in the face to wake me up. I am naïve and I must accept that for now, until I expose myself to a world of plentiful thoughts; positive and negative.

I stand up after my thoughts come to a good conclusion and jog back home. After about nine or ten minutes, I reach home and run straight to my room. Should I sit at my desk? Should I lie down on my bed? Should I rest on my recliner and stare into space? Should I like down on the floor and scream? What should I do about these thoughts? How shall I respond to this concept I have just acquired?

Overwhelmed with it all, I respond to my new acquisition in a way I am not accustomed to. I change my clothes, turn off the lights, and walk over to my bed. I lie down and sleep. I sleep at 5:45 p.m. It is the oddest way in which I have ever dealt with new ideas and concepts. A transformation is clearly taking place. Regular is no longer regular; regular is deeper and darker than anything imaginable.

———————

I wake up at 6:33 a.m. and walk over to my shower, turn the water on, select my clothes from my closet, and get in the shower. I feel refreshed, I have slept for a long thirteen hours. I feel like a bear emerging from a cave after hibernation. While showering, I bump against the wall, trying to make a beat; then I sing. I sing the first lyrics that come to mind—something completely insignificant, about running miles for love.

After my spontaneous morning shower, I change my clothes, eat a protein bar, brush my teeth, and leave my room. I then walk back into my room, take a pencil out of my drawer, open to any page in one of my notebooks, and write: *I don't know what it is, but I wanna flee it.*

What is this? Is it melancholy? Is my world flipping upside down? Is something tearing my world apart? Circumstances are good; everything is good. I did not write those words for no reason. It is like I have a second writing conscience that is different from my mental conscience, and this writing conscience is aware that something is wrong. I trust it; something is wrong. Too much is being installed all at once without being checked. My thoughts and feelings feel like a cell that continues to produce malignant cancer cells.

I return home from school and go up to my room, perplexed by the traffic in my brain. Am I damaged? What is this? Did I not just discover the presence of philosophy in life? *Open your eyes, Zach; see the overtreatment! Appreciate what should be appreciated! Write down what should be written! Cry out what should be cried! Direct what should be directed!*

I close my eyes to think, and I see darkness. Actually, I see myself in darkness, screaming. I am locked in! I open my eyes, shaking. Has writing been taken from me? Am I now locked in with my thoughts; has my time come? I run over to my desk, and take out a pen and a notebook. I try to write on a fresh new page, but it isn't that easy. I try to write through it all. I try to write even when my mind will not allow me.

The only thing I manage write is:

> Massacre, I face it. I need to be away from it. However, I am the reason for it. Run away from my creations? How can I possibly? I could try to write through it, if only my hand would allow it, if only my mind would supply it. My mind refuses to comply; aren't I the one who controls you? I will not stand for rebellion. But that is what happens when one has three minds. Comply with my commands I ask you; actually, I demand. But my mind does not; this is poison for the thought, nutrition is scarce now. You will be left to spoil and shrink, you will be torn apart. Just watch as it happens.

Something in me is falling apart; even my writing is refusing to comply. My mind is in disagreement with itself. I have no homework. The only option I have, even though it is 3:30 p.m., is to sleep. I go to my bed and rest, trying to put it all behind me. Hopefully I will sleep through the shaking. Hopefully when I awake, I will return to my regular self.

I usually sleep with ease, but I stare up at the ceiling for thirty minutes. My chest still hurts; my body still shakes. There truly is something greatly irregular happening. I get out of bed and go downstairs to the kitchen. I grab a cup for juice; my arm is still shaking. I can't stand it anymore; I take the glass cup and throw it at the ground. There is no response from anybody in the house.

I grab another cup and throw it at the tile, shattering it to pieces all over the kitchen floor. I hear my mom scream, but nothing more. I grab another glass cup and throw it in almost the same spot, with the same effect. Finally, they acknowledge my message. My brother and mother emerge from their rooms, come to the kitchen, and look at me.

"What is this, Zach?" my mother yells. "Why are you doing this?" Muaz just stays quiet.

"I don't know, Mama, good question," I reply. "Maybe it is because I love you guys and want you to see it. Maybe it is because I'm afraid of something. Or maybe I don't fear anything, and I want you guys to see *that*. I don't know."

I examine their faces as I talk. I watch for every twitch and muscle movement. I stand in the middle of the kitchen, behind the kitchen island, while they stand near the large wooden table. Beyond their faces, there is structure here. I am the center of attention. I brought them here with a call; they listen anxiously to my answer. They have no preformed opinions; none of this was thought out before. Any answer I give will determine their argument. They follow my lead. And where do I guide them? I guide them toward a greater system, one that bestows knowledge on them. I inform them about my fear, lack of fear, or love, I am a leader in a drive toward something greater. This resembles one of the most extensive systems and ways of life in mankind. It resembles the concept of religion.

For example, in my religion, we issue a call to prayer by saying *Athan*; people come from everywhere, scramble together, and form lines. In these lines, they stand and pray behind an educated man, a man who knows religion. To every word he utters, they respond in an organized manner. Hundreds to thousands to millions to billions of people follow a man and allow him to lead them. They move when he says the Word of God and end prayer when he does. But they are not worshiping this man; he is merely a leader, a leader of a greater cause. A leader who guides the people toward religion and moral conduct through prayer.

Imagine a system in which I governed people and led them toward a belief or a system. What if I were not just as a leader; that is belittling. What if I led people as a member of law enforcement or the government? Maybe—given my mind and my obsession with manipulating others for my own satisfaction—I was meant to tear basic human intellect to shreds and rebuild it on my terms, direct it toward a divergent, esoteric system. I am surely capable of causing an uproar and controlling the human minds; how can I incorporate that into real life? That is the greater question of mankind.

I snap back to my temporarily distorted reality. Muaz and my mother are still watching me, "This was just something I need to let out," I say. "I am sorry. I will clean it, I promise. And I will buy nice cups. Again, I am sorry." My goal is to relieve the tension in the situation.

My mom hugs me, which is very unusual, and says in my ear, "It is okay, love. Please, next time, try and let it out better. I am happy that for the first time in your life I am seeing you let out your anger."

"Please don't do anything like this again," says Muaz as he walks back upstairs.

After cleaning the kitchen, I go back into my room and sit at my desk. I feel refreshed and amazing. My mom is right: to let out my anger is a beautiful way of relieving my internal pain. It is nice to learn that sometimes writing is not the only solution. My ability to write is back; however, I feel free. I grab my pencil and write something short to start this new direction:

> You are all under me.
> Wait for the thunder and storm
> to strike your brains, kill your independence ...

P.S. Am I really back to normal? Look at the vision in my writing.

CHAPTER 4

The sunlight blinds my eyes. Driving at 2:00 p.m. is hard, especially when you hate sunglasses like I do. I am in an insane hurry; no time to do anything. The red lights are consume too much time; my thoughts, the scenery, my feelings—they all take too much time. However, I am on my way to success. I am on my way to the opportunity of a lifetime, to become phenomenal. *Shut up, Zach! This is not the time to think; just drive.* I will lose my momentum if I continue to think about the moment. But I have to live in the moment, live through it all, because this trip is for those who doubted me and for those who inspired me. This trip is for the dead and the living, for Wyatt and the people who are figuratively dead to me. My psychology has sustained me. My psychology put me in advanced placement (AP) classes and gave me an insanely high SAT score. My psychology kept me determined, even through my depression and self loathing. My psychology is the reason I am in the state of Connecticut, in the city of New Haven, driving to Yale University. I made it.

It took the belief that I was abstruse because of my kindled abilities. It took the death of a self-loathing teenager to stab me in the chest with anxiety, but more important, to teach me what I want to do. I want to write. I want to tell stories and show people that I am unique. I write about people who realize what life really is. However, I am describing my own life; all my stories are disguised descriptions of me. I cannot write about myself directly. Instead, I must demonstrate the mind of a revenge-seeking genius.

I've come to Yale to become a prodigy, to sell my soul as a writer. I understand that the determination I need here is one hundred times the determination I needed in high school. But I gave up my life for this. I gave up my friends, parties, social interactions, and technology that I do not need. I gave up everything for this. I told everyone that I would distance myself from them and their drama, because I was going to be something great. I abandoned people for this. And the most astonishing part is that nobody but my family knows I am here. Nobody knows that I made it, and I will not tell them until I have reached my peak of success, if I ever do.

The Yale campus is now in my sights. This is my new home. I will thrive here. I will work and work. However, I will always find time to write, to talk to papers and computers in my own words.

Pulling into the lot, I realize this is one of the most successful moments I've ever had. I feel great, because I've turned sadness and disappointment into something good. I made it. I open the door of my Honda Accord, step out, and close the door. I walk with precision, each step about a foot-length apart. Then I lay my eyes on of the most beautiful buildings ever created. Yale has existed since the eighteenth century. The walls, the roads, the fields, the students—all are wonderful to me. This is truly beautiful. After six years here, I will be a successful person, working toward getting a job. Thank you for not letting me hold a grudge. Thank you, mind and childhood, for not allowing me to dedicate my life to anything but myself and my work.

I can't wait until I get to my dorm and can write about this—how an isolated little boy not only tasted success, he dined in the middle of it. I will write tales of criminals and anguish, happiness and sacrifice; stories about people with emotional disabilities; soldiers who fight against intolerance; people who see life like as I do.

———◆◆◆———

I set myself up in my new life—campus life. I talk to the correct people, register for my classes. I am now an established person. My life, for the next six years, will be here. My roommate is reserved like me; he focuses only on absolute necessities. I can tell he is at this university because he never found a life outside academia. He is short and thin, about five foot five. He wears huge glasses and walks with a limp. A scar on his left arm extends from his wrist to about three inches below his bicep. He has this bony face and very thin dark eyebrows. He looks like he's had a lot of trouble making friends, so he's made schoolwork his friend. I ask him what his name is, and he tells me but I completely forget. I think it starts with a T or an R or something like that; it is on the tip of my tongue, but I just cannot get it out. It doesn't matter; I can ask him later. For some reason, despite my spectacular memory, I always forget people's names.

His name is Robi. I ask him so many times, I finally remember. The more I talk to him, the more I can sense his fear. I get this feeling that he is hiding from something; he doesn't have an enormous level of arrogance like many of the people on campus. He scratches at his head a lot, bites his nails, and does other actions that make him appear very nervous.

There are many different types of people at this college, and my roommate is in one of the main groups. First, there are the people who are gifted but only academically; otherwise, they don't seem that intelligent. They have a crazy work ethic, but they don't even know it, and they never need to extra motivation to convince themselves to work more. Second, there are the arrogant people, who are also academically gifted and believe that nobody is on a par with them. There are the people who were the valedictorians in their high schools, full of team spirit, and leaders in everything they do. If they die, there will be a documentary about their impact on those around them—everyone in town, parents, friends and family, teachers, and coaches. Finally, there is the fourth group, people who are subconsciously always motivating themselves to work. These people weren't "given" anything and got into Yale because of their work ethic and open-mindedness. They learn from the mistakes of others, and that is their greatest success. I wholeheartedly believe I am in the last group, but obviously I am much more philosophical.

Robi is in the first group, the intellectually gifted idiots. He has low self-esteem and is driven by only by his false belief that he is incapable of having a social life. He chooses work over friendship. He walks around with a weird, puzzled look on his face. He always seems confused, like he is constantly trying to differentiate between left and right. I wonder if he knows what happens in life, if he sees the news, if he has ambition, if he has anything but basic creative intelligence. He does not seem to be a follower or a leader. He is neither predator nor prey. He seems to be like the spotted algae-eating fish that sit idly for hours at a time, sucking on the aquarium glass. He has no personality; when we talk, I have this odd feeling that I am in a real-life utopia. I feel like I am living in a place where the government dictates what each citizen must be, i.e., a person who lacks curiosity, is not street smart, accepts the current situation, and never searches for something bigger. As time progresses, my vision improves, and I see something else in Robi.

I feel sympathy for him. His limp, the way he maneuvers and walks, makes him look crazy. But I can see past his disability. He works at an unbelievably fast pace, and once he is finished, he grabs some fruit, usually a banana, and sits upright on his bed. He sits on the bed, leaning against the wall, and reads for about an hour. Then he grabs his laptop and does some quick research, before watching, for about thirty-five minutes, online videos that are somehow hilarious to him. He laughs very quietly, chuckling in a low tone. After that, he turns off his laptop and stays quiet for about twenty-five or thirty minutes until he falls asleep. His days are all the same. And while he goes through his routine, I sit at my desk and stay up hours, studying. A perfectionist, I do my work with ease and check it repeatedly. I take many breaks and doze off all the time. I wish I was able to study as quickly and efficiently as Robi.

Today, I finish my work much faster. I write anytime I have free time—short stories, additions to my book, or notes. But today is different; I am exhausted. I want to throw myself down on the bed and live the easy life for a few hours. I sit down on my bed and watch movies on my laptop. Robi is reading yet another book, *The Alchemist*, which is about a searching for oneself. I wonder what a person like Robi thinks about as he reads a book like *The Alchemist*. What is his thought process? Does he feel motivated? Does he feel powerful? Is he proud? What is he is feeling? I can't keep wondering. I want to understand his unusual and intriguing mindset, the mindset of a creature of habit. I cannot accept that someone's brain can be so contained.

"Hey, Robi," I call to him. "Is that book good?"

"Yes it is a pretty good book. I kind of like it." He stutters every few words; he then looks back at his book. Okay. Well, this is an incredibly boring conversation, but I have to understand his mind. I have to get in.

"So, would you say the book is motivating or inspirational to some degree?" I ask, desperately trying to spark a conservation.

"The book is a story of a shepherd who goes on some adventures to find himself, to defy the law of shepherds," Robi says, calmly. "Why would I feel motivated by that? I am not a shepherd."

"You do not have to a shepherd to feel inspired by this book, Robi," I tell him.

"I don't understand," Robi says. "I've never felt motivated. I just do what I am supposed to do." He looks back at his book. Is he indicating that he wants to concentrate and that I should stop talking? Is he even smart enough to hint at things; does he have such a detailed mind?

"Oh okay," I reply. "Well, that is good I guess. I'm going to get back to what I was doing. Just continue reading your book." I am annoyed, but I smile so I do not seem too rude. I think he senses how I feel, though.

"Yea, okay, me too," he says.

I've wasted a four whole minutes of my day conversing with someone who is not even close to my superior intelligence. He is an extremely unkind person, unkind to his mind. He should entertain it more and serve its favorite food—visionary thoughts. I am unkind to my brain too, when I partake in such unproductive conversations and allow my thoughts to think about someone who is not worth my braincells.

When I realize I am thinking about Robi, I immediately want to halt my brain processing and think about something else. This is very hard to do. What causes me to want to enter his gray matter and comprehend his very thoughts? Why am I incapable of enforcing the law in my head that requires me to stop thinking about Robi? There is a rebellion going on in my head, I want to stop thinking about him; however, my curious braincells have different ideas. I know something; that is what it is. I have an overwhelming sense of mistrust. I do not trust what I see because I believe that there is more to Robi than the common perception of him. My senses have never been wrong; I am going to trust my gut. My gut has a brilliant history of being skeptical about others. Maybe it is the seven-inch-long, three-inch-wide scar on his left arm, his fidgety behavior, his comfort with the way everything is, and his lack of perceptual detail. Whatever it is, my gut knows something makes me to want to go after him, and I trust my gut. Zach Smith, you have never failed me; your intellect is unlike those in other humans. With open arms, I introduce you to a world of great intelligence and a mind that one day may control governments. Just wait and see.

———◆◆◆◆◆◆———

Yale university. Writing. Two different atmospheres enter in my head, depending on what I'm working on. Stress finds its way into my daily life because of my working schedule. I have been here for about six months, and the characters in my stories are dealing with an overwhelming amount of stress. My stories are like autobiographies, but in the strangest way—through the examination of morality.

Right now, I am working on a book about a boy named Ali who can control the world with his smile. He gets people to do things they've never dreamed about doing and spreads positivity, although he also has the ability to spread negativity at the exact same level. He is able to be kind and evil. That is the theme of the story.

Although Ali has the best of intentions, when he gets older, he develops bad habits, because a supernatural force talks to him and makes him smile. The force uses Ali's smile to create riots and enslave people. Everything feels wrong, and Ali is unsure about his destiny. One day, somebody tells him that life will be different if he becomes the supreme ruler. He puts all of his efforts into achieving this goal. He gathers people and smiles into their eyes, manipulating an entire nation. He tells them about his plans to control nations even though he is only twenty-three years old. Nobody opposes him and the only thing that can stop him from becoming a tyrant or make him become a magnanimous ruler is his conscience. The only thing that can block the supernatural force residing in his head is himself. His life as a supreme dictator is an unbelievable mixture of kindness and brutality. The book is about entering the mind of a mixed personality, about a person with the ability to be ruthless and kind—much like me.

It is when he slaughters a goat with his own hand that his desire for power changes completely. He watches the goat struggle and kick, until he smiles at it with his devious smile, and that that brings the goat to submission. The animal stops his attempts to save himself. Slaughtering the goat wrecks Ali, giving him desire to flee from himself. He is incapable of running away from whom he is, so he spends the rest of his life mired in self-loathing. He screams to the Lord day in and day out, and asks why he made Ali so proud that he believed he himself was God. The story ends the moment Ali no longer achieves happiness by tormenting souls.

Ali is me, exaggerated, of course. Ali's power is my manipulative capability. The goat is Wyatt, the boy who died when I was in high school. The cry to the Lord is the stigma of excessive pride, my vanity, my narcissism.

I still live in anguish because of Wyatt. It's weird to realize that I still think about him. There are nights I wake up screaming because I dreamed about him. My brain finds it hard to comprehend that I have gone to school with somebody, seen him day in and day out, including the day he died, and gotten the news that night that he'd tied a rope to the ceiling, made a knot strong enough to hold his neck without the rope coming apart. And then he ended his life. The thought of Wyatt's death penetrates my heart and smashes my braincells to this day. Wyatt, you are the goat; yet somehow the concept of the goat is the complete opposite of your suicide.

It is the opposite because I believed that, like Ali, I had unusual powers to control minds and people. However, the difference is that when Wyatt killed himself, he showed me how much power I didn't have. That is why I had severe depression and lacked self-worth. In the book, the goat gives Ali the ability to understand just *how* much power he has. People and animals give up their lives for Ali, which is the complete opposite of what happened to Wyatt. Although the ending was different, the result was the exact same. I wanted to morph into someone else. I wanted to run away from myself, to dismantle my soul. And so did Ali.

My book is beautifully detailed. It explains why a man would want to run away from his soul, the way he screams at God, terrified because his power made him think he was godlike, but death reminds him that he is a mortal. He has sadly forgotten that death would do its part and could do so at any time.

Once Ali reaches the peak of evil as an absolute ruler, he makes an entire nation suffer. But he doesn't want to fix what he has done. All he wants to do is escape, but he can't, so he spends the rest of his life hating himself. I don't think that man is always programmed to correct his wrongs, to create good due to excessive guilt.

In my real life, though, as everyone knows, I will be great. I will continue to write as I have for the last two years. Writing is the only thing I love to do anymore. The death of my anger and hatred for life is due to the tools I use for writing. So I will write on till death does its part or my brain is incapable of comprehending thought. Luckily, because of my brilliant mind, that is a long time away, unless I have a tragic accident.

———◆—◆—◆———

Muaz, my business savvy brother, visits me at Yale. I welcome him into my dorm room. As he walks in, he says, "We should go out and eat or something."

"Dude, you just got here," I say. "You haven't even got to see anything yet." I'm a little annoyed by his lack of interest in my campus life. "Like, you haven't even met Robi. This is Robi."

"Nice to meet you, Robi. I am Muaz."

"Nice to meet you too, Muaz," says Robi and goes back to his desk.

"It seems small, but life here is big. We work a whole lot, more than you can imagine," I tell Muaz.

He walks around to our little kitchen. "It is a nice little place that you two have here," says Muaz. "Hey, Zach, can I get some water?"

"Yes, of course you can. The cups are at your top left." He grabs a cup, opens the fridge, and pours some water in his cup." He walks around and looks around, reading the walls. I have quotes all over the walls—quotes from some of the great influencers in the world.

He walks over to my desk, lifts up one of my binders, and opens it. "Hey, don't read that, Muaz," I say. "I don't want anybody really seeing that stuff." With his dominating personality, however, he continues to read. He sits down on our brown couch and crosses his legs, reading some of my pieces. "Muaz, let's go somewhere or do something," I say. "Please leave those alone." He is really getting on my nerves, yet I try to be as polite as I can. I walk over to take my binder from him. But he says something that completely intrigues me.

"These are your notes, obviously," he says. "Why do I find them so disturbing? They are just notes." I stay silent because there is obviously more he wants to say. "These notes are talking to me; they almost make me feel guilty. I knew you like writing Zach, I totally did. I just never thought your writings were that good. If your notes are this good and this authentic with its voice, then this writing could be something terrific and huge."

"What do you mean, they are talking to you?" I ask. "Explain that to me. I don't get what you mean."

"Okay," says Muaz. "Well, here you write,

> Happiness—no, not that very commonly used word with a very insignificant meaning—but true happiness. True, pure happiness is gained when one goes through ultimate perseverance and achieves great success. When one gets kicked in the gut and sacrifices what it is that he or she loves, when they work in gruesome amounts and ultimately build their legacy as successful individuals. That is the purest happiness a human being can ever feel. Since this is the case, why does one procrastinate and slump? Why

does one settle for easy and live life with minimal effort? Why does one allow the distractions in life consume them? Is man hiding from happiness?

"I know it is just a note, Zach, but this voice speaks to me, makes me question my life, my drive. Your writing is authentic, and I want to read something bigger, something you've completed." Such emphasis is rare with Muaz.

"I have written many short stories," I reply, "but are you sure you want to read them, because they are not normal. They can be gruesome at times, maybe even ill-natured.

"Yes, I do," he answers. "Writing has to be [word missing]. I don't know much about it, but I do know that."

I open up my laptop, type in my twelve-digit password, and open a file—"Live Love Die." This short story is ninety-six pages, but the plot seems four million pages long. It is another story about Ali, the creative genius, describing how containing an untold story is agony for him. He searches for himself and for outlets for his creativity by torturing people. It is very gruesome, especially in the parts where Ali's methods of torture become spontaneous. Throughout the story, I describe Ali's past and his emotions, and the reason the story is because his past was not terrible. He grew up happy and complete; he was not neglected as a youngster. But he never found a way to express himself, so he found happiness in devising plans for drugging people, tearing families apart, hurting people in all ways, even killing people. By the end of the story, Ali decides that his actions are all God's fault, because God made it his fate to kill people for no apparent reason. Serial killers, people who committed wrongs, as Ali does in the book, are usually psychopaths, or there are other understandable reasons for their actions. In this story, I ask, rhetorically, why God created evil in the world, and I question God's sanity. The story is not intended for all audiences, which is why I didn't quite want anybody to read it, but

I need to hear some critiques. Given Muaz's tendency to forget about morality, he may be the perfect candidate to give me some feedback.

I print "Live Love Die" and hand him the manuscript. "Don't steal it, I will find you," I say, laughing.

"I don't know; I may have to," he jokes back. "Let's see how good you are. If this story really does have potential, I will let you know."

"Okay, that sounds good, now let's go out somewhere." I say.

He puts on his shoes, and I slip my feet into some black slip-ons. He opens the door and steps outside. I follow him, with a small gift box in my backpack. Muaz wears a light-blue dress shirt and a dark blue tuxedo jacket. He has slim, black dress plants and black Calvin Klein dress shoes. He dresses very nicely, as he has since he was about sixteen or seventeen—a tendency he acquired from my dad. In fact, he looks like a younger version of my dad. He is not too tall, just about five feet, seven inches, and has a chubby face and neck. It is obvious that we are brothers; however, we look very different. Our physical shapes and statures are very different. Our personalities are completely different. Almost everything about us is different.

We walk over to my car, my black Honda Accord Sport. I turn on the car, reverse, and drive to a restaurant about twenty minutes away. Muaz is visiting me at a special time in his life, but he has yet to tell me about it. When I called to invite him, he said that there was something very special he wanted to tell me. In the car, we talk a little about my writing and laugh about childhood friends and imagine their current lives. Conversations with my brother are always a combination of fun and seriousness.

At the restaurant, we order some appetizers. While we wait for them, I sip on my Sprite while Muaz drinks a Coke. I pull out my backpack and put the giftbox in the center of the table. "This is for you, Muaz. Open it," I say.

He opens it and sees a Hublot watch, an automatic skeleton watch. "I wanted to give you a present," I tell him. "We have been apart from each other, and I want you to remember me when I am at Yale and you are not."

"Zach, this is a Hublot!" He is shocked. "This watch is at least $15,000! I can't take this."

"No, you have to! I have some money on the side. Don't worry about the money. I just want you to be happy."

He gets up and hugs me. "Thank you, Zach. I love you, bro."

That is something I haven't heard in a long time—from anybody. It is nice to hear. "Well, try it on." I say.

He puts it on his left wrist and says, "I love it a lot." His smile is a smile I would pay a fortune to have. When we were children, I did not realize how much I really love Muaz.

"So what's the good news?" I ask, staring at him.

He looks back at me and says, "I landed the biggest deal in my life, I am now co-owner of a company called Machete Sails. We sell motorcycles for now but plan on selling nice cars and stuff in the near future. Zach, I'm twenty-one, and I will make about $300,000 this year. This company is going to be something big soon."

"Nice job. I knew you would hit something big soon. I always knew it."

"Thank you. We even named the company Machete Sails after you. Remember? You came up with that name in the car once, and I liked the spelling of sails and the idea of it, so I always kept it in mind. Thank you," he says.

Machete Sails? I can't remember coming up with that. And I also can't see Muaz retaining a thought like that; thoughts go through his head like water flows in a river. I guess I could be proved wrong.

"Thank you," I tell him. "That's really nice of you to remember something like that. How are you going to do this and still focus on college?"

"Well, that is the second thing I wanted to tell you," Muaz says. "I've dropped out. Think about it. I was at a community college while you are at Yale. I am not meant for college, like you are. My success will never come from school, because I can't learn anything there."

I have always believed everyone should go to school. However, he has a point. School is not for Muaz. He doesn't value education and ideas as he should. He never did well in school; he always just barely passed. He is extremely intelligent in business, but in every other subject he is average or even below average. He always seems to run away from school while I embrace it, despite my melancholy.

"You know what, Muaz?" I say. "I support you. You can do better than school. I wish the best for you, and I know you can do it." I say these words easily right now, but there were times in the past when I never could have told him something like that. I was so hostile toward him and undermined his abilities, because I always got the better grades and was always more capable. He proved me wrong. "I am sorry, by the way, for the way I treated you when we were younger," I tell him. "I sometimes looked at you as almost handicapped, and I really am sorry. You were always great at what you did." I have to get that off my chest because otherwise I will be overwhelmed by guilt.

"It's no big deal Zach," he says. "I love you, bro. We will start something significant and amazing!" He tries to keep me from feeling, which he does mostly by saying he loves me. It is very rare for either of us to say such a thing.

"I love you too, man," I say, smiling. "Let's eat."

Time goes by. Nights do too. I work for grades. It's all chaos in my head, Am I the only one? It sure feels like it. Robi is always on the other side of the room, working in his own quiet, seemingly carefree zone. I feel worlds away from him. What makes him seem so lifeless? And what in me that makes me believe he is scheming? Have I gone mad, or are my instincts actually sound? Can I spot abnormal personalities?

Is Robi motivating me to write? Yes, he definitely is. For example, he inspires me to put this poem down on paper.

> You are a wicked, merciless freak who deserves my respect and fear. You are wise and artistic and grossly underestimated.
>
> You speak to me all kinds of words; many of them seem to be lies. I sometimes see you drop to the point of insignificance; the result is happiness and madness. Unfortunately, I feel just like you do when you are low. You are so close to me, yet so far.
>
> Tear out my own eyes, you command? I will not! However, I may devise a plan to decide who receives what emotion, while quietly and gradually tormenting them all.
>
> It is regularity, I declare. There is so much more to it, you insist.

What have you been feeding me? Why does nobody else eat this? All you tell me is that you feed me what no other human being is fed. Stop limiting me to such basics; free me from this chamber. I am no amateur; tell me all I need to know.

Stay mysterious if you like, but I will reach the core of your reasoning. You're closer to me than you think. I have so many different varieties of you. I will find and embrace you by using you as a tool.

Oh intelligence, don't we have such sweet conversations?

Robi, I have no choice but to trust my thoughts about you. I wait to return to normal thoughts about you but time does not always heal all, although information sometimes does. I am sorry to tell you this, Robi, but I will expose you to both of us. Let us hope that nobody else gets tied up in this, because I will not halt my plans for anyone or any reason.

I call to him. "Robi," I say.

"Yes?"

"I have been wondering, what is your mother like?" Again, I try to spark a conversation.

"Why do you ask?" asks Robi.

"Well, we should get to know each other," I reply. "I have been around you for months, and we will together for even more time."

"Okay," Robi says. "She is a nurse; that's all there really is to her." I notice a faint hint of defensiveness in his tone, something that I could potentially feed on.

"Well, my mom was a pharmacist for a long time," I say. Maybe if I open up to him he will return the favor.

"That's nice to know," he says. "I'm going to get back to work though." He's basically telling me to stop talking. I will give him time, I am a patient manipulator.

I get back to my own work. There is a dryness to his speech that agitates me.

"Have you ever feared anything?" I ask him.

"Feared anything?" he replies. "Why do you ask? What do you mean?"

"Well I fear myself sometimes, my father sometimes, and my mother sometimes," I say, assuring him that it is okay to be afraid.

"My father died when I was twelve," Robi says. "I don't fear him. My mother was a nurse. People don't fear themselves. That doesn't make sense. If you fear something in yourself, then just change it. You can do whatever you want to yourself."

Is he telling me that I don't make sense when I am clearly trying to encourage him to get personal with me? I'll show him.

"I'm sorry about the loss of your dad, Robi," I say, looking deeper into the objective and not the little insignificant comments.

"Well, it is okay," he says. "It is not a big deal."

Death? Death? Death? Death isn't a big deal? Death depresses spirits! Where is the sanity in this man? "I'm sure it is a big deal," I say, a little offended. "He was your father, not a random pedestrian."

"We were close but not superbly close, so his death didn't hurt me that much." Robi lies down on the couch. What the hell is wrong with him? My leg is shaking, my heart is pounding, my chest is breaking. Wyatt Kimmel was not my dad, but his death ended my life. How could his father's death not have an impact on his life?

"Well, what about your mom? How is she doing?"

"She is fine. She is a nurse."

Is he programmed to answer any question about his mother that way? "Do you call her and check on her often?" I have never seen him call his mom, and I am with him a lot.

"Not really, no," he says. "She is doing fine. She has her nursing job."

Does he not realize that he has basically repeated the same phrase three times in two minutes? "You don't call your mom at all? You don't care to?"

"I do care to," Robi says. "I just haven't had the time and stuff. I'm going to get back to work now."

"You don't have work," I say with irritation. "You said you were done with everything fifteen minutes ago."

"Yeah, you are right," he replies. "But you should get back to work." He is right. I should get back to work. I have some work I need to finish up and I would cannot stand hearing him speak right now. Robi may be the closest thing I have ever seen to a lack of a conscience.

I open my laptop back up, open a file, and get back to the essay I was writing twenty minutes earlier.

———◆◆◆———

I bite into the barbeque chicken pizza that I ordered. I eat this same pizza about three or four times a week and never tire of the taste. This pizza tastes so good. "Hey, Robi, would you like some?"

"Yeah, sure Zach, thank you. I am starving." He gets up off his chair and sits on the couch, and we eat together. Robi has never really done anything to me. I have known him for nine months, and he has been peaceful all along. However, as I sit with him on the couch, I can feel myself getting angry at him.

"My close friend died when I was in high school," I say. "He killed himself." I thought Robi should know something about me that is private.

"Well, I am sorry to hear that," Robi says. "But he chose to die; that's what he wanted. Everybody does what they want, so it's not that bad."

I can't reply; for a minute or two, I am speechless. Finally, I ask, "Do you have any siblings?"

He says, "I have a sister. Her name is Keke. I haven't seen her in a while however. We just don't talk much, you know?"

No, I don't know. I don't understand how someone could not speak to his mother or sister especially since his father is dead. "How old is Keke?" I ask.

"She is sixteen."

His sister is not an adult. She is a teenager, and he doesn't speak to her! Who told him that, since his mother is a nurse, she doesn't need anything from him? Not even love and compassion? "Have you never loved anything or anyone?" I ask him. "What the hell is wrong with you? Have you no humanity, no heart?"

"I do, Zach. I just have school and stuff. And my mom is a nurse," he says. He takes another bite of pizza.

"Your mother is a nurse? Your sister lost her father! Where is your heart? My mom hurt me emotionally all the time when I was young! She committed wrongs that I will never be able to forget! However, I call her every day, and I always check up on her. You are not supposed to give up on your family!" My tone becomes increasing assertive, and my voice grows louder. Eventually, I am screaming.

"All right, Zach," Robi says. "Calm down. Listen, I am done eating. I will get back to work and try to call them later on." He tries to sound reassuring.

"Hey, dude. I am not telling you to do anything. It is your life. Don't move out of your comfort zone." I feel as though I am killing my pride.

"Okay then, I won't," he says. "Thank you for clarifying your intentions." He sounds more serious than sarcastic. But how can he dismiss an idea that quickly?

I want to punch him in the face, this is a person without soul, without a conscience. Damn him! He makes my insides hurt. I feel helpless. I will never talk to him about anything other than education. Robi is like a robot, a product of artificial intelligence.

"I am going to get back to work too," I tell him; except I don't get back to work. I get to writing.

> What were you thinking? What were you thinking when you left emotion out of some of the humans you created? God, do you desire injustice? Did you put people on this earth to suffer? You say everything happens for a reason, so tell me why at times I consider inflicting pain and hurt on people, and at other times I can't live with myself because of the guilt. Guilt without reason. Guilt I cannot live with. Guilt that depresses my spirit and torments me. If everything

happens for a reason, tell me why you allow people to live in constant agony. Tell me why you took the souls out of people. Tell me why you allow people to die inside without actually allowing them to die. God, I fear you more and more, because you psychologically torment people. It is hard to believe everything you do is for a good reason when I see people go through agony that lasts lifetimes. I can't love you when I know how much you terrorize people. You are the sole creator of injustice in this world. How can it be just when you make people fear themselves, when you take away people's desire to live. Justice and injustice are in each person's psychology, and you take sanity away from people.

I write with anger, with hurt. My words take me back to the days when I was hurt, and I went insane after choosing to filter out my anguish through writing. Robi is heartless; however, it is not my role to judge him. God made him; allow the Creator to deal with the creation. Unjust or just—that is not for me to question. I write stories about real life.

———————◆◆◆◆◆———————

Perspective, you have lied to me once more. You have deceived me. Whenever I convince myself that I know it all, a supernatural force slaps me in the face with a wakeup call. Robi is not a heartless person; he has a soul. I am wrong to see him as soulless. There is something strange about him. However, I never could have imagined what happened to him.

We are working as usual, each person in his designated study area. I finish writing down some notes for an upcoming test. I walk over to the kitchen to grab a drink and a paper towel to clean up the rice I've dropped on my desk. I open the can of Red Bull and drink from it. I stand there, just gazing, thinking about my notes.

All of a sudden, Robi starts screaming. He grabs his purple notebook and throws it at the wall. He is shaking aggressively. I go over to him and ask if he is okay. He says, his voice cracking, "My mom is a nurse. Why did she hurt us like that?"

Did Robi really just say that? Is he having an emotional breakdown? This is the oddest thing I have seen since I entered college: somebody without emotion is having an emotional breakdown. I grab him hard and tell him not to think about her. He says in a croaking voice, "I can't stop. Ever since you brought her up, she is all I can think about." I see blood pour slowly down his face. His eyes are bleeding!

This is not a game; this is a terrible thing. Robi's eyes are bleeding. He is crying blood. But why?

"Robi, Robi. How can I help you? I don't know what to do." I am a bit scared. I have never seen anybody cry blood and shake with such intensity.

"My blood pressure is very high," Robi says. "We should wait this out. Just calm me down please."

I hold Robi in my arms; this is the toughest scene in my life story. I keep repeating "it will be okay" in the most soothing voice I can generate. The paper towel is saturated with blood. I don't know if I should call the police or continue to hold him. He seems to have gone through this before, so I think he has an idea of what to do. I wish I could tell him about how much blood there is, but that would be unwise.

"It will be okay, Robi. It will be okay. It will be okay." I say over and over until he returns to normal. I take him to the bathroom and wash out his eyes.

"Thank you, Zach. You handled it well. This doesn't happen unless I am extremely stressed or too deep into thought. Don't ever bring up my life and childhood again, please. It bothers me a lot as you can see."

I feel so guilty. This was my fault; I should have blocked out my thoughts. I should not have attempted to understand Robi or to interrogate him. "I am so so so so sorry, Robi." I say. "I swear I am. This is my fault." I am genuinely apologetic.

"It is okay, you did not know," he replies.

"No, no. I am very sorry." It is wrong to allow my thoughts to become actions like that. Robi does not deserve what I put him through. Containing my thoughts is something I need to do from now on.

Robi walks over to his desk, sits on his chair, and starts writing again. I am shocked. "You are just going to get back to work, as if nothing happened, as if we have not just spent the last forty-five minutes stopping you from crying blood." I am shocked beyond all measure.

"Yes, I will," Robi says. "That never happened. Never bring it up again." he says.

I wish I could do ask he asks, but it is not that easy. He cried tears of blood because he thought about his mother. I thought Robi was composed only of academic intelligence and nothing more. Tortured souls can be the ones who appear the farthest from it.

CHAPTER 5

The pictures on the wall have such pure intention; their intentions however are the only good things about them. The smile I see on my face when I look at them does not warm my heart but reminds of a lack of unity. The pictures on the wall depict my childhood, so that, sadly, is what comes to mind.

As I've grown older, my hatred for life and my childhood has become less apparent. I do not spend as many hours thinking about my motivations or compromise as I used to when I was growing up. As an adult, I should only feel gratitude for my childhood. These pictures on this wall have a provoke a physical reaction. They don't feel like regular, smooth glass; they feel like shattered glass. My fingers hurt when I touch the pictures, as if they have smashed into the glass, although the glass appears to be intact. These pictures give me a tingling feeling of betrayal. I feel wounded when I look at them. I wonder how my parents got me to smile; that must have been a very tough feat to accomplish. *Zach Smith smiling as a child? Was this Photoshopped?* Seriously, this cannot be real, I was dark, quiet, and gloomy. These pictures do not reflect who I was when I was young.

I already want to leave this place. I hate looking at those horrid pictures of the wall. I loathe this house. Maybe visiting my mother and brother was not a good idea. Actually, it was a terrible idea. I do not want to experience my childhood again. This house is dark and demonic; it represents every emotion I felt in my teenage years.

Tearing apart the walls and burning down this house would soothe my mind and heart.

My mom walks out of her room, past the kitchen, and into the living room, where I sit. "Mama, I missed you a lot," I say, getting up to hug her for the first time in over a year.

"I missed you too, Zach," she says. "I wish you were not at college."

"I know, Mama, but education is the only way to achieve success in this day and age—and not just from any Oklahoma college or university. I intend to be profoundly successful. Always strive; Dad taught me that." I giggle when I mention my dad, because I know how much that irritates her.

"No, Zach," she says. "I taught you that all your life. Your dad is just an animal doctor." Though the good of the world is in my dear father, she never can allow herself to admit it. She always wants to take credit for everything positive. She has a sense of entitlement that makes her tough to deal with, especially because I am exactly the opposite. I lack any understanding of wanting to take credit for everything around you.

"How did you get here?" she asks. "Who drove you from the airport?"

"I came with Muaz; he is coming back in about twenty to twenty-five minutes. He went to go get some food." I reply.

"You two could have told me," she says, making her best attempt to sound convincing. "I would have cooked for you guys."

I laugh. "Mama, with all due respect, I haven't seen you cook in years, even though you always say that you will. Buying food from a local restaurant is not such a bad thing. It definitely saves us time, you know?"

As usual, she takes offense. She is offended by everything anybody says. Ironically, when we were children, she scolded us for getting defensive when people criticized us. Now, she has the dire need to defend everything she's ever done.

She tries, but fails, to hide her agitation. "I actually cook every day now. You can ask Muaz. He stops here every day to eat. And my friends—they all love my food with a passion." Well, that is funny, because Muaz is the one who has told me she still doesn't cook. I did not make it up. I don't want to argue with her. I have only been here five minutes, and we are both already agitated.

"Actually, Mama, you are right, I was just joking with you. Muaz and your friend Ban told me your cooking is great." I try to sound pleasant to resolve the situation. She gives me another hug and says, "I will be back, I am going to change."

I don't know where her agitation comes from, but mine derives mainly from my current environment. I so badly want to escape. I had the same feelings when I was younger man—anger, regret, fear, melancholy, and, surprisingly, vanity. This household is where I bottled up every emotion I ever had. I never had any way to expressing my emotions. I wish I'd had the ability to deal with them, especially those strong ones that I encountered when that bastard Wyatt killed himself. I am sorry, *Wyatt, that just spilled out. I meant no disrespect to you or your everlasting legacy.* By legacy, I mean the gift he gave me—an outlet for my thoughts.

Wyatt introduced me to writing when he died. Before that, writing was something obligatory I did for school. When Wyatt killed himself, writing became so much more than that for me. Writing was like an invention. I never had a way to express myself, to really feel the pleasures in life, until I came across the concept of pouring my thoughts onto a blank piece of paper. Everything I ever loved was forsaken by this terror of a system called life. Now, years after

Wyatt died, I recognize that the true inspiration for my writing was Wyatt. I never truly appreciated him for what he gave me. *Your legacy will follow on.* In fact, I should find out today just how far my legacy will go: Muaz told me he had some news about my books. He will be home now any minute. Today I will find out if the only thing I have ever truly loved and believed in—to the point that I sacrificed my glorious smile, my love for this addictive world, my fun in manipulating minds, my social life, my entire life for—loves me and respects me the way I love it.

My mom comes out of her room wearing a pink dress she's had for about five years. I remember the day she bought it. We were in a small shop in Cairo, on one of the oldest streets there. I was drinking guava juice, and Muaz was reading a biography for school. He despised reading that book; he spent our entire trip complaining about that book. Meanwhile, my mom tried on dresses for forty-five minutes. My boredom was so intense that it has been barely surpassed since. I also remember that day so well, because we saw a different version of my mom for the first time—an outgoing, stylish mom.

She's come to light several times since I left Orlando. But when I was in Orlando, every time I visited her in Oklahoma City, she was like that. She used to take us everywhere. We sometimes went to see the beautiful orange Oklahoma sunset by the water, which was my favorite view. Damn, change can be so significant when one gets what he has been longing for, as my mom did when she took us from Orlando. I wish mankind did not adjust so fast; it makes us forgetful and unappreciative of what we have. I wish failure and anguish were deeply engraved in our minds, so that once we achieve success, we never forget the feeling of failure.

That dress represents one of my fondest memories. Maybe a lesson I have struggled to learn is that there is good and bad in everything in the universe. In other words, not every memory I have in this house is one of pain and struggle. I have very pleasant memories in fact. In the eighth grade, I wrote a story about my plans to singlehandedly terrorize nations and trash the intellect of man. The suspension I got was worth it. I loved every minute of I reading it aloud to my classmates. It is a fond memory, because I let out previously concealed emotion for the first time in my life. There are indeed good parts to life, despite my feelings of dread. I wish I could thank God for it; maybe one day my little mind will give me the passion I need to thank him for everything. Maybe. But for now, I dwell in a state of skepticism over the creation of this earth. For now, I sadly am not an appreciative man.

In addition to the pictures on the wall that symbolize the deception of our childhoods, there is even a more disturbing scene in this house. It is a perfect representation of hypocrisy. The words of God are written in calligraphy on the wall to my right—excerpts from our Holy Book. They never held any meaning to me, until one day I took a picture of the calligraphy and showed it to a guy who could read Arabic. He told me they were verses from the Quran, specifically from surah (chapter) al-Ma'un. I looked up surah al-Maun and read it carefully. My heart hurt. I felt hypocritical and filthy when I read those words:

> Have you seen those who deny the recompense? For
> that is the one who drives away the orphan. And does
> not encourage the feeding of the poor. So woe to those
> who pray. Who are heedless of their prayer. The ones
> who do to be shown. And withhold simple assistance.

Those words are so elegantly written on the wall, yet we don't pray, and I often do good just for show. In fact, if I am completely honest with myself, I do everything in the hope it will be seen. My entire life has revolved around manipulating people and showing them that I am great and powerful. When I write, I write for doubters, for my family and friends who underestimated me. I have no will to do good things for a supernatural power, for God. All I ever wanted was to flourish in the eyes of people, to control them. How can these words sit on our wall, warn us not to love the world too much, and yet we continue live our lives peacefully? This household is corrupt and shameful. Everybody will see what happens to the little boy who came out of this house. They will see him achieve great, unheard of things while they bottom feed like catfish. My house is filled with hypocrites, except for me, of course. I am excluded because I was not taught any better.

My brother walks in, puts the food down on the kitchen table, and takes off his orange sweater. "Food is ready" he says. I walk over there. I feel light-headed. My stomach is growling. I am so hungry. Chinese food is just the thing. I grab a chair and sit down with my mother and brother. "Thank you for the food, Muaz," I say.

"Don't mention it," Muaz says. I take a bite of the food, and as I chew, Muaz says, "I have good news, Zach. "I want you to believe every single word you hear because this may not sound very believable."

"I will try," I say, anxious to hear what he has to say.

"I sent your stories to a huge publisher, Garden Oaks. The head of the company loved them so much that called me personally and begged me to let him publish your book."

"Are you serious?" my mom asks. "The head of Garden Oaks? They're huge; they are basically a household name." My mom is bewildered.

"Yeah, Mama," Muaz says. "Zach could get tons of recognition for his books. All I hear is that he is immensely talented and that he writes like he is a great published author," says Muaz, hyping us both up for this deal. I stay quiet, deep into thought.

If I publish some of my short stories, will a lot of people read them? No, probably not; my stories are meant for a special type of audience. I am surprised that so many people like them, as Muaz says; my stories are a little aggressive. But if I do publish this book, I will receive something amazing. I will be able to release my thoughts, my ideas. I no longer will have to live in a world where I must contain my thoughts. Isn't that what I've always wanted—to have an outlet, a way to express my thoughts and feelings, my sorrow and gloominess, my happiness and love, my obsessive need for control and my vanity. I could release everything I think and no longer have to live with the pain of not expressing myself.

"What do you think, Zach?" asks Muaz.

"Yeah, sorry for being so quiet," I say. "I was just thinking. And, yes, I do want to do it. I want to publish the books and sell them. I want to make a life out of this." I am grinning. I feel a special, rare type of happiness—the type you can't pay for. My heart feels light.

"Then let's do it," says Muaz, as he eats another bite of the chicken.

My mom looks at me and says, "You might do good. Try hard." She seems so stilted when she says it.

"You can't even show happiness at a time like this?" I ask her. "Everything I have done in the last few years has been focused on writing, and now that I learn that my writing is great, you won't show any genuine pride." My palms are sweating, and I can feel myself getting agitated.

"Well, people say that all the time," she says. "Just finish college and focus on academic things. That is all you are capable of."

"Whatever!" I say. "I wish things like this never happened, because of you."

"Watch your mouth!" she yells at me. I shut up and look down at my food, I am still hungry, but my appetite is completely gone. When my appetite goes away, there is no bringing it back.

My brother and mother finish eating, and I go to the bathroom to wash my hands. Muaz walks in and pats my shoulder. "Do not listen to her. You will do well with this. *We* will do well with this," he says.

I grab him and hug him tightly. "Thank you," I say, meaning it more than I know how to make it sound. I really do appreciate what he has done for me, and he knows it. I let him feel it by appearing vulnerable. In reality, I don't care what my mother has to say; she has been negative since day one of my life. It just agitates me sometimes that she does this and then smiles in my face twenty minutes later, making anyone that opposes her seem crazy.

"We've had dinner with her," I say. "I am going to head out. I will go to the mall to buy some clothes and then catch my plane back to Yale."

"Okay, just hug her before you leave, so everything is left on good terms," Muaz says.

"Of course," I say. I walk into the kitchen and say, "I am leaving, it was nice visiting you Mama."

"Yeah, it was," she says. "You seemed a little unkind this time, though, more than usual."

I don't acknowledge her comment, stepping on my pride in order to do so. I hug her stiffly. "Bye. Love you," I say as I walk out the door. I unlock the door to my rental car, a 2008 Chevrolet Impala, and get in. I turn the keys and look out the window to see Muaz standing there.

"You were going to leave without saying bye?" he says, laughing softly.

"Sorry man. I didn't mean to. I love you big bro. Let me know what happens with the book."

"I will. Love you too," he says.

I roll up the window and reverse out of the drive way. I look back at the house once more before I leave, feeling fairly emotional. On the trees are the cameras that we put up but never use, which is basically our family in a nutshell—potential never used. I drive off, feeling a tear run down my cheek. I haven't felt like that so long. I really do love this house. I try not to think about it, because I want to hide it. The house raised me well, and for that I forever will be appreciative. I whisper under my breath, "I love you Mama." I want to go return, badly, but I can't let my emotions cloud my judgment. Back to Yale University I must go. I drive on.

◆━◆◆◆◆━◆

Three of my short stories published by a major, successful company, at least that's what I hear. My life is going to change. I will be wildly successful, that is, according to Muaz and Garden Oaks Publishing.

My three stories are all released at the same time. Three weeks pass, however, and I don't see much success. I don't know where the people at Garden Oaks get the crazy idea that my books will be successful, but I am told to just wait and believe. *What makes my books so different?* I ask. They give almost the same answer every time. For example, Jonathan from Garden Oaks tells me, "Your books have a defiant voice in them that compels the reader to read on, religiously. It is almost impossible to stop reading them. They are compelling to a degree we have never seen. Give it a few more weeks, and you will sell faster than you ever imagined. Things take time, especially if you are new at them."

Apparently I will become a great author, and I have written enough to sustain me for a while. But I cannot stop writing. I must continue on. I must strive. Yale is hard on me; writing is harder. But I have proven to myself that I can succeed at both. Nothing can stop my drive. I have a 4.0 GPA, and my writing soon will be on bookstore shelves. I am more capable than I thought I could be.

Isn't this all I have ever wanted? Hasn't God given me everything I have ever wanted? Deep inside, I know it is true: I have been given the world. However, on the outside, I will not admit it. I will not allow myself to credit any of my success to a supernatural being, because I am too arrogant and self-absorbed. I worked for all of this, hours on end, so it is all mine. Nobody has given me what I have. I've earned everything because of my extraordinary work ethic.

I do not want to be a hypocrite. My writings defy the Lord of this universe. They scold him; they blame him. I can't be so hypocritical that I defy him in words but thank him in actions and emotions. For I fear my self-awareness more than I fear God. My mind reminds me about my wrongs when I commit them and terrorizes me day in and day out. Nothing is more traumatizing than my own self, I promise you that. The guilt I have felt throughout my life impairs me.

I wake up Tuesday morning, and go to class at 9:30 a.m., as usual. I take notes, preparing for my test next week. Pre-med has been hard since day one, but after some time, I got used to it. I get home from class, lie down for twenty minutes, and then get up and walk into the kitchen. I microwave some noodles, add lime and hot sauce—something Sarah and Mia taught me how to do—and then start eating. My phone rings. It is Muaz. I swallow the food and answer the phone. My nose is stuffy, so I blow it really quickly, as he is on speaker, and then say hello.

"Hey, Zach," says Muaz. "I am on the phone with Jonathan and Mona at Garden Oaks. We are on a four-way call I. We have some good news for you and wanted you to hear it."

"Hello, Mr. Smith, this is Jonathan. Your book *Live. Try to Love. Die* has gotten great nationwide attention the last three days. Some people have gotten their eyes on it, and sales are blowing up. This book is going to be a *New York Times* bestseller very soon; we are talking, in the next week or so. Your other two short stories have also received some attention, but not like *Live. Try to Love. Die.*"

"I cannot believe it; somebody please pinch me so I can know that this is true!" I say, excited and laughing.

"Mr. Smith, this is Mona. Can you tell us in a sentence or so what this book is about? We need a very short summary, so that we can redesign the cover. Because a lot of people judge books by their covers."

"Well, in short it is about a man who is living the sanest and most comfortable life. Then, like glass, he shatters abruptly, without reason. In the wake of his destruction, he spends days and nights crying out to the world. The more he cries out, the more devil-like he becomes. The book is a first-person view of the death of one's sanity and happiness, in the most gruesome and relentless way. It is one of the more defiant books that I have written; it questions the fairness of the world and the justice of God himself. The storyline is not as long and mind-boggling as other books; however, the voice of the character gives the book a charming and enchanting effect." I try my best to summarize it, but it is pretty hard because to me the storyline is much more profound than that.

"Okay, Zach, keep your head up and your eyes out. These sales are ready to dominate the world with a vengeance," says Muaz. He has been hanging around these publishing consultants too long; he is starting to sound like them.

"Okay, bro," I say. "Thank you, guys. Call me whenever you have any news. Bye." We all hang up.

Everything around me is changing. People in school have been noticing. People I have met at different points in my life are reaching out to me. Everybody sees it. I am becoming iconic. My book is selling well worldwide; it has broken sales records. People in school come up to me and ask about my books; suddenly, they all want to know me because I am an "accomplished novelist." My life is taking a different direction. My need to satisfy others, my obsession, is being fed. I now can manipulate others with such vigorousness. I now can control others in a way I never would have imagined. Maybe this is what has been destined for me, a boy who only ever truly wanted one thing —to control other people's minds, to wrap people around my finger and control them like puppets. Maybe that is the whole reason that I will fade faster than I rose up. Maybe I will be so obsessed with my pride, my need for control, that I will lose everything before I am able to grasp it all.

For now, I know three things: First, people want to meet and know me. A lot of people who never cared to contact me are now blowing up my email and phone. Now they suddenly want to be around me and see me. Second, I have broken many sales records. My books, especially *Live. Try to Love. Die*, are changing the world of books as we know it. Third, something in me is vanishing gradually, that is, my need for acceptance. That is an emotion that has haunted me for a long time, although I have tried to block it out. I have believed it had gone; it had not, but it is truly disappearing now. I have what I have always wanted. Slowly, I am becoming less dependent on what others think. Success and borderline fame are virtues.

My brother calls me; I pick up the phone. "Muaz, where are you? Did you rent the car yet?"

"Yes, I did," he says. "I am on my way to the restaurant we ate at last time I was here. I'll be there in thirty minutes. Meet me there."

"Seven Swans Steak and Sushi? That restaurant?" I ask.

"Yes, that one," he says. "Be there in exactly half an hour please. Bye."

"Bye, Muaz," I say.

That restaurant is only ten minutes away, so I have about twenty minutes to get ready. Can I take a shower and put on something fancy in that amount of time? Yes, I can. I can shower in about five minutes and spend fifteen minutes getting ready. I already have my outfit ready: my navy-blue blazer, light-blue Calvin Klein dress shirt, slim-fit black dress pants, blue patterned Perry Ellis tie, and black Calvin Klein dress shoes. I grab a towel and turn on the hot water in the shower. I brush my teeth in the few minutes it takes to get the water hot and then get in the shower. I expose my hair to water and apply olive oil shampoo and conditioner—the best kind of shampoo and conditioner for softening my nappy, curly hair. I stand there and sing for about a minute; then step out. I spend about four minutes drying and brushing my nappy hair and then change. I put my socks on and go over to the bathroom and spray myself with Versace cologne. I have to look my best for this dinner, because my brother is with a well-known television director. I check the time and still have fifteen minutes. I leave so that I can settle myself and prepare for Muaz and the director's arrival.

I get in my 2013 Chevrolet Camaro, enter Seven Swans Steaks and Sushi in the navigation system, and start to drive. I arrive at 6:47 p.m., about five minutes before Muaz.

"Hello, how may I help you, sir," says the girl at the front desk. Her nametag says Jennifer. She is tall—about five foot eight—and pretty. When she smiles, her face glows. She has dark-brown hair, green, plant-like eyes, and perfectly aligned white teeth.

"Hello, Ms. Jennifer, you look very good today," I say, flirtatiously.

"Aww, you do too sir. You are very well dressed," she says. "Do you have a reservation or are you just walking in today?"

"Well, you clearly assumed, probably because of my suit, that I have a reservation," I say, laughing. "Yes I do have a reservation, under the name Muaz. He should be here in about five to ten minutes."

"Okay, sir, let me check that for you." She types his name into the computer. "Well, we have your seats right here; let me walk you to them." She walks me to the table. "Wow, you are much taller when I am standing next to you," she says, clearly attracted.

"Call me, Zach," I say.

"Okay Zach. Here is your seat. May I get you a drink?" she asks.

"Well, Jennifer, I'll just wait on the rest of my party," I say, smiling into her delicate green eyes.

"Okay, Zach. Well, I'll get back to the front. I'll bring your party back when they arrive."

I spend the next few minutes playing games on my phones to kill time, which is not typical for me. Usually, I like to write, but I find it hard to write on my phone. I look up and see Muaz walking in, wearing a nice suit; directly behind him is a short Caucasian man, his long brown hair in a ponytail. They are guided by Jennifer, the waitress. She points them toward my table. As she turns away, I meet her eyes and wink at her. She giggles and looks down at the floor. As Muaz and the director walk to me, I stand up with my back straight.

"Zach, this is Mr. Mahone," says Muaz. "He's directed some of the best-known television shows in recent years. Mr. Mahone, this is Zachariah Smith, a great, great author."

I shake hands with Mahone, and he smiles and says, "Huge fan of your work, Mr. Smith."

"Likewise, Mr. Mahone." I say, which is a white lie because I do not know who he is. My brother has not mentioned his name before.

Mahone has sharp, piercing blue eyes. His smile is mischievous, yet compelling. He seems eager to sign me to something, I can tell by his stance. He walks behind Muaz, trying to appear innocent before he bashes me on my head with some offer.

"Zach, Mr. Mahone is about to change your life," Muaz says. "He has come all this way from Los Angeles to tell you about it." Muaz seems more excited about this deal than I ever could be.

"Mr. Smith," says Mahone.

"You can call me Zach," I say, interrupting him.

"Okay, thank you, Zach. Well, I came all this way to talk to you about a project we want to pursue. As everybody knows, your books are getting nationwide attention. Your writing voice is defiant and intelligent in a way that we have never seen before. Your writing is extraordinary. As a director, I want the world to be able to see into your mind. I want to create a reality television series that gives the audience the ability to enter the mind of a philosopher, a mad master of words, as we call you at the office. This will also promote your other writing and put you at the height of the writer's world, which you will control with your fingertips as you've described in your stories."

As I predicted, Mahone looks innocent but his words are powerful, cunning, and well-articulated. But I am not one to fall into traps of others with manipulative words, so his words don't weigh an ounce on my scale. I and the life I see for myself are the only things that compel me to make this decision. I will sell books at a musical pace. I will cause an actual uproar, bigger than anything I have previously done. Mahone is not exaggerating; I will control the writing game; I will flourish among the greats.

Before anybody can say anything, Jennifer comes over with a little notebook and a Sharpie pen. "Would you like to order anything to drink?" she asks. She comes at the perfect time. It bothers me that Mahone starts talking business the second he comes in. Usually people wait for the mood to be set; this guy is too persistent.

"I'll take a mango juice," I say.

"Okay, one mango juice for Zach," she says, smiling at me.

"I'll take a Pepsi," Muaz says.

"Okay, one Pepsi," she says, without any enthusiasm. She is clearly trying to show me that I get special treatment.

"I will take a Pepsi too," says Mahone.

"Okay then, two Pepsis," says Jennifer, almost snobbishly. "Well, Zach, your drinks will be right up," she adds and then walks off.

"I can't express to you enough how this deal will benefit your writing," Muaz says. "I really do like the idea." says Muaz. He is evidently unable to grasp the concept of privacy; not all conversations should be held in front of other people.

"Let's order food," I say, after a long pause.

"Okay, let's wait until she comes," says Mahone.

His business strategy annoys me, leading me to question his skill as a director. "Well, Mr. Mahone, tell me a little bit about your work. You clearly know about mine fairly well," I say, breaking the silence.

"I've directed some of the biggest names in television and some of the biggest movies," he replies. "Have you heard of *The Plaza, The Casual Entry, Torn Apart by the Wind, Mark's Fantasy, The Crybaby of Las Vegas*? Well those are some of my works, and there are many more of them."

"Yes, sir, I have heard of them all," I say, astonished. "Those are big-league names. It is very nice to actually meet you. "

"I am sorry that I did not properly introduce myself," says Mahone. "I can tell that is why you were a bit hostile earlier."

"No worries, sir," I say.

"No need to call me sir," he says. "Call me Julian. Don't make me sound too old." He laughs, and Muaz and I laugh with him. "Your brother is a great entrepreneur," Mahone continues. "He really knows his business. He's worked tirelessly to set this deal up and cares a lot about your success. You have a great brother."

"That is very true. Thank you, Julian." I look at Muaz and say, "Thank you, brother. You are the kindest soul I have ever met." Muaz reaches out his hand, and I give him my hand to shake.

"Thank you, Julian. Thank you, Zach," Muaz says. "Now let's get down to business."

Jennifer returns, carrying our drinks on a silver platter. "Thank you Jennifer," I say softly, touching her arm and smiling at her. I can feel her attraction toward me, something I have not worked to appreciate for a while.

"Don't mention it," she says. Her eyes twinkle like a beautiful night star. She hands their drinks to Muaz and Mahone and asks, "Well, Zach, what would you like to eat?"

"I am not sure. What do you think is best?" I reply to engage her in conversation.

"A twelve-ounce, medium rare steak sounds great to me right now," she says. "Ours are the best." she says.

"You just read my mind, Jennifer," I say. "You have excellent taste. I'll have that."

"Okay, I'll put that in right now, Zach. What would you guys like to eat?" she asks. They give her their orders, and she walks away. We get back to talking.

"So … how would the reality television series process work, Julian?" asks Muaz.

"Okay," Mahone says. "We'll fly a camera crew to your home and start shooting as soon as possible. We'll pay you about $280,000 per episode, if we get the ratings I expect, which is very likely to happen, given the show's character and my connections with the media."

"That is a crap-load of money," says Muaz.

It is true; that is a decent amount of money to start with. And this show will promote my books and get me on the map. I am destined to become famous.

"Will there be extra drama needed for each episode, or how will it work?" I ask. "I do not want to become an actor in this television series. I want everything to be authentic and unplanned. I am a novelist, not a Hollywood actor." I speak deliberately, to express my point.

"I completely understand," says Mahone. "You will go through your regular daily life; we will show samples of your writing. We will interview you at multiple points in each episode, and you will reflect on your thoughts and opinions. It is up to us to make the show appealing to the public. Making TV shows interesting is a talent I have, just like you have your writing talent. All you have to worry about is living your daily life, even if that means sitting at a desk all day." He makes it sound like it is no trouble at all, when in reality I am selling my soul.

Jennifer comes with our food, and we start eating. After several minutes, I break the silence. "Julian, I'll do it. And as I clearly will make money from my writing and in this new television series, I am going to drop out of school." I have just made a life-changing decision; only time can tell whether it is a wise one. I reach out my hand to shake Mahone's and say "Let's do this, Julian and Muaz." They both shake my hand; all three of us were happy, at least for the moment. This could be the beginning of a most destructive path.

I go to the bathroom and wash my hands. As I walk out, I see Jennifer and call to her," Hey Jennifer, can I get the check please."

"I will be right there." She brings three separate checks and hands them to each one of us. We all pay separately. My meal is $37.26, mainly because of my addiction to natural juices. I asked for six refills. I put down a $65 tip to make her day. She grabs all three checks and walks over to the register. In two minutes, she comes back with our cards and receipts. "It was a pleasure serving you," she says and walks away.

"Well, I will be seeing a lot of you, Julian," I say to Mahone. "Bye for now."

"Bye for now, Zach," says Mahone. He walks toward the door.

"Where will you live now?" Muaz asks me.

"I will move to LA," I reply.

"Okay, good. I have to go too, Zach, Bye brother. I will see you soon. Thank you."

"No thank you, Muaz. You are very kind, I will see you later." I hug him, and he walks out behind Mahone.

I grab my blazer, put it on, and walk out. I wave at Jennifer and go outside. I walk over to my Camaro and open the door. Somebody calls to me. "Zach! Wait up!" It is Jennifer.

"Hey," I say, astonished to see her.

She walks over and hugs me tightly, "I don't normally do this, Zach. In fact, I never have. But you were so kind and generous in there. Thank you."

"It is my pleasure. You are beautiful and a hard worker. I wanted to thank you for that," I say, taking advantage of the moment. Her green eyes look into mine, and I can't help but smile. I am returning to my old ways. I was a fool to try to avoid who I am; there is no escape from it, unfortunately.

"Zach, let me have your number. Maybe next time I won't be the waitress," she says with a chuckle. Her laugh is inspiring, divine, and cute, and she has perfect teeth. I give her my number and she says "Well, I have to get back to work. She hugs me and I hug her back.

I whisper in her right ear, just like I used to do, "You're gorgeous."

She pulls out of the hug and looks at me and says, "Bye, Zach." Then she kisses me straight on the lips, just like the girls used to do. People really don't change. Now watch as I dismantle her heart, just like old times. As she jogs back inside, I smile like I used to. I will never change; silly me for thinking that. Now watch as I rise from this locked chamber.

CHAPTER 6

Four years later …

The pages are scattered everywhere, all over the streets—scattered just like the minds of those who read them. Did you know pieces of paper can affect the composition of gray matter? Yes, I am serious. People use these papers I have written as methods of survival. How? Well, they memorize every single line I have written; then they translate those words into real-life meanings, because when I write, I use fiction. I develop characters and put them through hardship or good times and show people in my books how they react to every problem and the way their brain processes. My stories are meant to signify real-life difficulties and issues, so people from all over the world chase after my lines and form their own opinions about what each line means. Then I watch from the sidelines, (as a sports coach does) as their brains slowly undergo changes until they become walking reflections of my stories. Don't believe me? Do I sound boastful? Yes, I may sound boastful, however, take a twenty-minute walk outside, and you will witness for yourself walking, breathing, living forms of characters from my stories.

Lately, I have revolutionized the world of writing. My books have sold at such a quick rate that, for the first time in recent history, I have surpassed the sales of all the best-selling songs combined. I singlehandedly control the writing world. Three of my books are among the top ten best-selling books of all time. Other than the religious books, my works have been ranked as the most thought-provocative works the world has ever seen. People hail me as something other than human at this point, because I am so powerful and intellectual.

They call me a prophet, someone directly associated with God; luckily, those are the extremists. Among regular people, I am known as a brilliant philosopher who expresses his ideas in writing, specifically, short-form fiction, books that are between ninety and 110 pages long. It has come to a point in which I symbolize a God-like brain capacity. I have all the time I need to myself; all I do is write. My reality television show came to an abrupt stop after four years; now I spend my days putting together billions of letters to express affection in the only way I know.

The big question is, why do my books sell so well and influence people the way that they do? What makes my stories so special? It is because I destroy minds and then rebuild them on my own terms. I motivate others to follow their dreams. I give my readers a strong sense of self-worth, even if it did not exist before they read my words. I convince men and women from all over the world that they have undiscovered abilities. I am able to this so successfully because every word I write comes straight from the depths of my heart. My writing is emotional and genuine; it appeals to the weak and the vulnerable, the strong and the incapable, to regular, balanced people and to those who need help. I write this all from my heart, because I tell the stories I wish I'd been told as a child. I wish I'd been told that I was capable, that the skies shined in my name, that the heavens opened up for me, that my intelligence is unlike that of any other man. I was never told these things; instead, my motivation came from hatred for others, which made my drive for success so bitter and persistent. I love to see people read my books and cry due to the intense motivation they feel. I connect with them, because that is all I ever wanted to do. "Give what you were never given," my father once said to me. I live by those words.

I also have this intense tendency to shake men's intellects, to watch them crumple like cookie crumbs. I love shocking people with concepts of how this world can carry evil; shocking them because my characters believe and revere God, yet they scream at him in the middle of the nights. They blame him for torture. They say,

> Dear God, you are there. It is known, and you took a sane man's sanity from him. Watch me with your constant gaze as I fall on my knees, bleeding in my heart, weaker than any imaginable element. As you watch me, remember that you have done this to me. You took from me the life I used to live and never gave me the ability to retain it. Justice? No, this is not justice. You allowed the demons to enter my soul as you watched with laughter. But who am I to try and make you feel guilty, for you will never feel it. I must suffer without opening my mouth to illustrate my pain. I am sorry, my dear God, for having spoken at all.

In sentences like these, there is deep intensity and aggression in the character's words. In other sentences, characters praise God with a calm tone, showing their love and appreciation for him. My books taunt the nature of man's morals. They affect the balance of choosing between right and wrong, thus trapping them in constant spirals. I found a way to manipulate human emotions and people's vulnerabilities, which I incorporate in my books.

I disarray the people's emotions and logic, so that they return to me with vivid intrigue. All people want is to read my books. They idolize me, they study me, they celebrate me, and sadly, they worship me.

Isn't this what you have always wanted out of the world Zach?

———————◆◆◆◆◆———————

Hand prints on the mirror. Breath fogging up the glass. Look in the eyes. What is it you see? I don't know.

The color red shaded into the face, heavier with every progressing thought. Muscle-tearing smile. Origin? Unknown. Then define this recurring, unbearable smile! I can't find a dictionary containing it. Damn your incompetence!

Internal tone pugnacious. Well, block it out! I try, I try. Try harder! Lower gaze. Mollify pain, momentarily.

Wrongs? None known anymore. Gratitude? For what? No reason to have any.

Glances of the past. Heartfelt smiles in all directions. Expressions of love and care—evaporated. No more happiness. Butchered heart. Blackened by the light? Indeed, do not trust those who appear to be enlightened.

Hostility becomes a first reaction. Mind was once a sanctum; now it scorches.

Common word: *was.* Everything in the past is now useless. The present fails to advertise the future; no sentiment in time.

Seventy-degree-angle, leaning on the mirror. Forehead pressed against.

Guilt silences all other feelings. Good? No, for this type of silence is evil. Silence caused by sharp knives; guilt becomes dominant.

Satisfaction with life comes to an end. Death of the heart; complete shutdown. And finally—withdrawal from the pain, utter silence.

Light appears. Innovation. Momentum. Survival from melancholy achieved.

Power to man's emotions. Love, passion, sacred repellent of despair.

Carving of paths, apparent nobility.

Same smile; different cause. Same smile; more damage. Attracted to one.

Loved; was mistaken. Dependence; anger. Same smile; different nature.

Forgotten; love no longer a factor. New direction. Back to innovation.

Character control. Success.

Fall. Plummet from the very top.

Again, standing at the mirror. Seventy-degree angle. Breath fogs up the glass. Define this smile! Same orders. Forehead presses against mirror. Lack of supervision.

Realization; this is life; vicious cycles of downfall and quick rise.

Same smile; naïve nature. Sanity.

For the first time: balance. No complete rise, no complete downfall. Balance.

Appreciation. Kindled heart. Social competence. Affection.

Live. Create. Dismantle. Combine both. Die. Happy ending.

———————◆◆◆◆◆——————

These men, they stand up and gaze at life, in an attempt to understand—even remotely—its beauty. They want to understand the construction of this planet, the beauty that enlightens the faces of billions of humans. Life is full of beauty to the eye, the heart, and the soul. Life is mesmerizing; so much so that it is a tragedy when men fail to acknowledge and reflect on the world's beauty.

How is it inside the world of a man born blind? Can this blind man ever appreciate the world and its marvelous beauty? Yes, a blind man does learn to appreciate, but in an entirely different way. He muses about the beauty of his own beautiful internal world, one he's crafted himself, a world that sustains his happiness. But occasionally, he has thoughts about the real world, which is what he truly wants to see. It is the Holy Grail compared to what he visualizes internally. So occasionally, he wonders about the beauty of the world he does not see. When this blind man does so, he sees unimaginable beauty, happiness. *This world must be full of winsomeness*, the man thinks to himself.

But what if this blind man is given sight and can see this beautiful world? He will be amazed. He will have excessive pride in the greatness of this world. This former blind man will see perfection with his new sight, but only for a while. It won't be too long before he forgets the pain of being on the other side, of being blind. It won't be too long before his appreciation disappears. It won't be too long before his eyesight is blinded again—this time, however, due to a lack of appreciation, as is true of every other man. Man's greatest disability is his inability to continue to appreciate something once he has grasped the idea of it and breathed into it. That is why our hearts lose their comfort.

I feel like a man who longs heavily for something and receives it. A man who aches and dreams, of a concept—to aggravate people's minds and cause them to turn to me. All I've ever wanted is for the people to see something in me, to see the concept put into life of a person who was intellectually gifted. I wanted people to see greatness in me, so I strived for it. I worked for greatness when I was a teenager and young man in a way that could not be comprehended. I stayed awake for days and nights, glaring into a screen. I even worked through my writer's block. I worked with the motivation that I knew one day I would fly so high I would touch that sky. On days in which I felt undermined, I envisioned revenge. I had a passion to achieve a prodigious level.

Now I realize that all I have ever wanted was attention, and I was willing to overturn every rock and search every grain of sand to find some. When my mother apologized for not giving me enough attention, it did not mean anything to me then, but it does now. I see it all now. I understand it all, every enraged emotion I have ever felt. All the narcissism I possessed. No matter how much I tried to hide from it—behind a desk or anywhere else—in the back of my mind I always knew that I r desire attention.

I was a boy who had an overwhelming desire for attention and satisfaction and was willing to work for it. And I got it. I was given the attention I wanted my entire life, on a whole different level. I received fame, more attention than I could ever imagine. I got everything I'd ever wanted. I possess a gift that has been given to very few.

From the outside looking in, one might question my passion. One might think of me as the blind man—given what he longs for, he forgets to appreciate it. But the most astonishing gift I've been given is an undying passion—one that is unlike any human characteristic I have ever analyzed.

For this reason, no matter how much success I achieve, I will always be in pain. I will always feel shallow and work at a compulsive rate. Memories of those who undermined me play in the core of my skull any time my motivation dies. That's why I stand up on stages with such authority, watching with pride as I dominate the minds of others.

My agent, Manny, stands at the bottom of the stairs. His sunglasses sit on top of his Los Angeles Clippers cap. He wears hefty black striped dress pants with a blazer and white dress shirt. He has a sparkling blue tie and a dark-brown expensive belt. He wears sophisticated clothes to appear "legit" and wears the cap to show his California spirit. We often argue about whether or not it is disgraceful to wear Clippers, rather than Lakers, accessories and clothes. He always tells me that he is a fan of the Clippers team because they win. My argument is that the Lakers are the real natives of Los Angeles, the core of the city. Sports can bring people together, like they say, but it can also drive them apart.

"Get down here," Manny says. "We have a show to get to, Zach."

"I am almost ready, give me thirty seconds man," I say.

He stands in the foyer of my 22,000-square-foot home in Beverly Hills. My agent is very good at what he does. He knows how to keep me intact and sustains my fanbase; however, I do not always cooperate with him. It actually agitates him sometimes, because his job is to sustain and increase my fan base, and I sometimes go against his orders. Sometimes I say what is on my mind and ridicule the fans; I make them appear vulnerable and naïve when I speak my mind. That is what agitates Manny the most.

I come downstairs with a blue Nike shirt with the logo drawn across it and gray basketball shorts with a red stripe going down. I am dressed like I am going to play a game of pickup basketball in the gym. My hair is brushed up as usual, and my teeth are clean and fresh. Typically, one doesn't dress like this to go a large event held in his honor, but I am unique. I could not care less; as they say, this world is mine and everybody else is just living in it.

"That is how you're going to dress?" asks Manny. "Come on, man, this is a big thing."

"Manny, I dress how I want," I reply. "This is what I feel comfortable wearing. Don't worry about what I wear, okay?"

"All right, it is up to you," he says, surrendering. He grabs the key to the Jaguar, and we walk outside.

"Man, the weather is nice; the classic LA sun," I say, in an attempt to start conversation. He seems down for some reason, unlike the annoying, elf-like creature I'm used to. "So we are driving the Jaguar F type today? Not the usual Bentley or Ferrari, huh," I say.

"Yes. The F type, you are the one that wanted to buy it, so I took care of it for you," he says, a little less monotone this time.

A question about the car was the perfect question to ask him; he loves cars. By asking this question, I am using my gift to control others and play with their moods. I want to engage him in a conversation that will make him happier. "I saw them, those Capuchins," I say, as we get in the car.

"You saw them? What do you mean you saw them?"

"Well, I researched them for like forty-five minutes before I slept yesterday. The stuff I read was pretty cool. I researched them, because I know you like them and want one as a pet."

"That is nice of you," he says. "How did you know I was interested in them?"

Now this question is my access into controlling him. "You mentioned it once a while back, like a year ago, but I remembered it. I remember everything you say, Manny."

"I … I … I didn't know that," he says, clearly flattered. "I always think you are not concentrating or thinking about more important stuff."

"I do think about a lot of different things, but I always leave space in my mind for you, man," I tell him. "Although it doesn't always appear that way, I hear everything you say and know what you are thinking too."

"Well, thanks, Zach," Manny says. "That means a lot. What made you think about the capuchin monkeys? You know they are the most intelligent monkeys in the New World, right?"

"Actually, I like them a lot," I say, preparing to say something that should make his day much better. "I bought you one as a gift of appreciation. It is a white-faced capuchin monkey. In fact, it should be delivered here in a week and a half."

"Damn, you bought me one! But Zach, how will I find time to take care of him?" He exhibits both gratitude and genuine concern.

"Well, I am going to build an extension onto your, something like a toolshed in your yard, a place to keep him in that is playful." This is all unplanned; I am making up these plans as I go. "I also will have someone come every day and take care of monkey, so that he can be occupied throughout the day. This way, he will not become aggressive when you do see him."

"Man, thank you." He hugs me, although he is driving seventy on the highway.

"Try to keep us alive too, just a little tip," I say, laughing.

He laughs too. "You really can work wonders with your money," Manny says.

I feel myself tense up; I am getting agitated. My chests quickly. Any joyfulness in my mood slowly vanishes. I hate nothing more than talking about money. "Don't ever say that again or I will be unable to control myself," I say as my face gets red. "Money is nothing to me. Money is not what gave you your stupid, pathetic monkey. It was my kindness. I don't think in terms of money, and you should never talk about my money like that near me. I do not do this for money, and I don't care to have any of it, not even one dollar. I never think about money, because it is damaging, and I hate the sight and presence of it." My anger is clear.

"Okay, Zach," Manny says. "I did not mean it like that, I am really sorry. I should have known better than to make such an amateurish comment." He tries to calm me down; instead, he makes me more furious. Saying that he should have known better than to make a comment like that suggests that he has thought that in the past. Thoughts about my money go through his head, which is even more infuriating. "If you asked me for all my money right now, I would give it to you," I tell him. "All I do is try express disgust when I am its presence. Don't you ever think about me in a materialistic manner or I will lose all my respect and love for you as a manager." I look straight into his eyes with my most threatening and vicious look.

He lowers his head down with deflated pride and says, "I am really sorry, Zach."

Manny controls my events and attendance, and he sustains my fans. However, if Manny ever interferes with things that he shouldn't, I put him back in his place, because I basically control him. I do not mean to sound possessive; however, his comment truly agitated me.

141

He clearly exposed my soft spot. I pat him on the shoulder and say, "Be prepared for the capuchin, okay?"

"All right," he says.

"I am loving this Jaguar ride," I say. "How far are we from the arena?"

"We are seven to nine minutes away," Manny says. "You will see it soon, Zach," Manny says.

I have reconciled with him to sustain my image of sanity but, more important, to eliminate any thoughts that he may have about finding a weakness in me.

We pull into the arena parking lot. My VIP spot has been set perfectly. I step out of the small coupé car, and four men walk around me—two in front and two behind. They escort me into the arena.

I stand behind the stage; I have not yet walked on. This should feel as natural and seamless as it always does. I just want to this event to be over. I grab the mic and walk onto the stage.

In the middle of the stage, I look to my right. Millions of people are screaming at the top of their lungs. "Zach Smith! Zach Smith! Zach Smith!" These are a small portion of my fans, from all over the country. They stand here to celebrate my presence; they idolize me. Most of all, they love me, although they have never truly interacted with me, and I do not know them as individuals. I only know them as two things—numbers and victims. Staggering quantities of people admire me; they are victims of my reign, my one-man possession of their minds. Yet, these people love me. The concept is still difficult for me to grasp, despite all these years of fame. I still do not quite understand it. And the greatest tragedy of all is that I do not love these people. I view them as fools.

People with fame credit their fans for their success and constantly remind them how much they love and appreciate them. I, however, I do not credit anyone else for any of my success and fame, which came from excessive agony, struggle, and work. My success and fame developed because of my intelligence and talent. I owe nothing to my fans.

This is probably why Manny has trouble with my attitude. This is why I stand on stage every time with my mind, but never my heart, because I do not feel their hearts flying through the air magnificently like I apparently should. For that reason, I will be able to write and achieve massive success, because the only time my heart is involved is when I actually write, and I write to those who undermined me and pained me. When I write, I channel my distaste with myself.

I grab the mic and say, "Hello, ladies and gentlemen. I am Zach Smith, as I am sure you all know. Let's get this started!" The crowd roars. I look straight at them and smile, as they smile at me, but our reasons for smiling are different. Whoever desires to comprehend the reason my smile at this moment, here is a tip: think about having totalitarian control without any empathy.

CHAPTER 8

The leather on the couch feels inflatable. The hot tea burns my tongue, a burn that will unavoidably remain on my tongue's taste buds. The fire warms the body but sadly, not the heart. High ceiling, massive walls, quality furnishings, beige walls, prominent chandelier, crowned civilian. Mimicry of time; a great failure to sabotage my stride. Dependent on an ever-growing supply, therefore, satisfaction rightfully should be a result; however, not in this world.

I sit alone in my living room, furnished with elegance in every direction. The clothes I am wearing are clothes I could never have afforded before. Money does not make happiness, they say; I live the truth of those words. Money has given me dissatisfaction and ultimately driven me to edge of sanity.

My sanity is no longer as efficient and dependable as it once was, for it is accustomed to fading out. My sanity is deprived by this vicious cycle in which I am trapped. The vicious cycle began with my discovery of an antidote for my depressed spirits, i.e., writing and selling my work. I felt gratification when I wrote, but that gratification was stolen from me again and again, so I keep writing. I live in a phenomenon of rotations of temporary happiness.

I had a drive throughout all these years of fame to keep writing. I had a reason. I wanted revenge for the times that I was accused of being a narcissist; that is why I lived to write. I used my passion for writing in attempt to mask what I'd gone through, and at times, it did work.

Lately, depression has gotten the best of me. Self-loathing has become a regular occurrence. They say loneliness and silence can make a good man convert. I was never affected by the pain of loneliness; lately, however, it has been aching my emotions. I feel lonely. I have nobody truly by my side. And damn, when the night falls, I feel like crying out to God to take me out of my misery.

I sit in this living room and stare, ponder. I retrace memories, I idealize my life. I experience happiness and sadness here in this living room, depending on my state of mind. I sit here a lot; sometimes I love sitting here, and sometimes I utterly dislike it. I look toward the kitchen and call out, "Mary? Come here please."

"Yes, sir," Mary says. Mary is my housekeeper. She has been looking after my house for about a year now, and she does a mighty fine job of it. She cooks whatever I want, and she keeps everything clean, which is actually pretty hard because of the shabby way I live.

She walks slowly; she is a slow-natured person and also kind of chubby. Her looks do not serve her very well; she is more intellectual than she looks. It takes her a couple of minutes but she comes to the couch and asks, "Mr. Smith, what would you like?"

"What is there to drink?" I ask.

"Well, Mr. Smith, one of your friends brought you a gift. Normally, I would have put it in the gift room for you to look through later, but you were not home, sir, and I did not want to put in there because it did not belong. The gift is a very expensive bottle of wine ..."

I cut her off. "Throw it away, I do not want it in my house."

She looks puzzled, "Excuse me, sir, are you sure? It came from one of your close friends, and it is very ..."

I cut her off again; I can feel myself getting agitated. "Listen, I do not drink, that is wrong and I cannot do it. Ever. Put that drink away, and I never want alcohol in my house again. Is that understood?"

Then I continue, "Sorry Mary, but what is there to drink in the house? Something I can drink."

"Mr. Smith, there is orange juice with pulp, just as you like it. Would you like that?" she asks, gently.

"Yes, that would be great. Please bring orange juice with a warmed hazelnut chocolate sandwich for me to eat. Thank you," I say.

"No problem, sir, I will bring it right up," says Mary. She walks toward the kitchen. I can tell she is bewildered by my reaction to the wine, and I honestly cannot blame her. After a year of living in my house, she knows I am not religious. She has never seen me pray or heard me bring up God's name. So it is quite understandable that she is taken aback by my reaction.

She comes back to the living room with the orange juice and sandwich on a tray just as I requested. She plants the tray down on the table, smiles at me softly, and says, "Would you like anything else, sir?"

"No, thank you very much, Mary. I am sorry I responded like that, but it is a sensitive topic for me," I reply.

"No problem, Mr. Smith," Mary says. "But since you brought it up, may I ask you about it?"

"Yes, Mary, you may ask anything. You know I always value your opinion on things," I reply, kindly.

146

"Well, Mr. Smith, I am not saying there was anything wrong about your reaction at all. In fact, I respect you for it, but I must say, it was a bit abnormal. May I ask, why you don't want to drink? Sir, you told me yourself that you do not value religion, because of your mom, and also you are known for being defiant of religion. I just would like to know, out of curiosity, Mr. Smith. If you do not want to answer, I understand."

"Well, Mary, your mind is actually my favorite thing about you. The question makes sense, and if I knew how to directly answer it, I would, but I can't. The only thing that I can tell you, which is very weird for me, is that maybe I actually value God, despite what I have said before. Maybe there is a part of me that is not utterly swayed from belief in him, as peculiar as it sounds. That is the only thing I can say." I am shocked that I am having a conversation like this.

"Okay, Mr. Smith, thank you for listening to my question, sir. If you don't want anything from me, may I go to sleep?" asks Mary, with humility.

"My pleasure, Mary. Yes, you should go to sleep, I will need your help tomorrow, which will be a big day for me. It is getting pretty late, it is almost 1:00 a.m. Goodnight, Mary," I say.

"Yes sir; see you in the morning. You should get some sleep too, if you have a big day tomorrow." Mary walks out of the room and toward the elevator. She presses the button and waits for it to take her to her room.

I direct my eyes back toward the fire and ponder life as I usually do. If I were able, I would most definitely sleep, but unfortunately, I am an insomniac.

<hr />

The next day begins with a huge, early morning event to promote myself. My agent, Manny, stands at the bottom of the stairs, hollering at me to hurry, as usual. "Zach, millions of people are either going to be there or watch this. C'mon!" Manny says.

"I got it. I am coming now," I reply, with less enthusiasm than normal. I am not looking forward to today's show. I usually sustain some joy when I go to these events and book signings no matter how I feel; however, today I do not feel joyful.

I walk down the stairs and fist bump Manny, "Let's go," I say. He grabs the keys and I follow him. He walks over toward the BMW i8, a car I have been wanting to ride in for quite a while now. "So, we are driving this baby today, huh?" I ask, engaging in a conversation to allow him to express himself.

"Yeah this car right here has ..." he stars with his yapping. I know I asked the question, but I cannot stand to listen to even one sentence of it. I feel pretty agitated, although I do not know the reason.

We reverse out of the driveway, and drive off to the airport. We will fly in my private jet to New York City and drive straight to Madison Square Garden for one of the biggest events of my entire career. This highly anticipated and organized event will celebrate my sales records. This trip will be very unpleasant.

At the Garden, I stand up on the stage with a massive, familiar grin. I'm the notorious writer that everybody wants to see. All these people are screaming my name at the top of their lungs. I'm standing here on a stage with millions of people so content about seeing me that it's like a plague. These people really do love me; why can't I love them?

I grab the mic and look around, I look everywhere, glancing in all different directions before I open my mouth to talk. These are human beings with working hearts and brains. At times, I seem to forget that.

I am here for a reason. They want me to talk; they want to hear the same horse crap they usually want to hear, and that's about my book.

They want little presentations about how I perceive life, and they want to question my book characters.

Normally, I would find it simple to speak at an event like this. This time however, it feels different; everything does not feel as it usually does. I feel totally stressed. I don't want to discuss my stories and my life. I want to explain to them, thoroughly, what this "dream life" they perceive actually is—behind the castle walls.

I look around slowly, swallowing the feeling of the atmosphere around me. I am not going to introduce myself as I usually do, with hype and enchantment. This time I abruptly say, "Have you ever had this overwhelming sense of guilt that smashing your frontal bone into a brick wall repeatedly wouldn't give you a three-second break from feeling your heart shatter each second? You may think you can run from it, but you're so tormented that your guilt won't let you escape. There is no relief from the searing pain in your chest. Your guilt wants you to be very alert so that it can agonize you and depress you."

The crowd gasps when I say this, and then—silence. There is no noise; only pin-drop silence. My talk is clearly too aggressive, but I truly cannot keep this in. The pain is overwhelming.

"That is how a man who supposedly has it all feels. There are no moments of genuine happiness. I'm always doubting what hoax the guilt and hatred are up to now," I say, passionately. It feels good to let it out. The crowd is still silent. I look over at Manny. He stands under the tunnel on the side of stage, red as a tomato. He verbally attacks me with whispers. I know he does not like this; I know it well. But how can I overcome this guilt when I fear for my image, when I'm a coward?

"You people can never comprehend what I go through!" I say, passionately. "They say ignorance is bliss; if only you people could understand the importance of those words. You are ignorant, and I urge you to stay that way. This guilt I feel is hell on earth. I wake up every day and feel devils walk next to me. I feel like I am one of them."

I lower the mic down near my waist. The whole crowd is quiet, Manny keeps yelling at me from the side of the stage, but I lift the mic anyway, and I go back to my speech, "My agent wants me to stay quiet about this. I can't. I won't. This guilt has exceeded my capacity level. I've matured and I've grown. I am no longer that twenty-year-old, trying to get my books sold to feed my vanity. I feel guilty, because I ruined human minds. My books have caused you guys to walk around dumbfounded, doubting the creations of every element of this world and why everything is how it is. Your minds are insignificant; that's how we were all created. We were never supposed to analyze the world with defiance like this. We were never supposed to analyze the authenticity of the wagging tail of a dog like this; it is a destruction of our fundamentals. My books have broken the filter on mankind's minds; they have smashed it to bits. There is no filter. How can I live knowing that I am a major cause of rebellion in the world?"

I take a pause. The entire crowd is still completely, utterly silent. It is hard to comprehend the conception of pin-drop silence in a crowd of tens and tens of thousands of people. I start again. "You people have endorsed books that eat alive the compassion that humans are supposed to have. You have lost your minds, and so have I. I lost my mind. Ladies and gentlemen, I stand here now to tell you all that I am a hypocrite. The most potent hypocrite who walks this earth. I say all this crap about defiance of life, God, religion, and stories; yet I don't fornicate. I talk; yet I don't drink or smoke. And there is only one logical reason for that, and it is because I believe in God, and I fear him. I fear this superior being, the same superior being I spent so many years directing distaste toward and plucking love for him from people's hearts. I'm a tyrant to the intellect. I am a hypocrite, and I do not fear to tell you!"

I look straight at the crowd. I have just dropped the jaws of tens and tens of thousands of people in front of me and millions of people all over the world watching this live. And perhaps, by the end of the night, I will reach a billion people, because of the massive Internet influence that we have.

Then it hits me. I know it all now. I open my mouth to tell the crowd. "Ladies and gentlemen, I have not come here to manipulate you into buying another product of mine. I promise you that. However, I do want you to know that I am writing something new! I want to write exactly what I've just told you. Scorn everything else I have ever written, because to me, it is unimportant. I will show you people what real intellectual despair is, not through fictional stories, but through my point of view. I will give you an in-depth description of the emotions of the human heart—the positive and the negative. I will show you what education can never show you. Let me introduce to you to the heart, down to its densest tissue. Just watch me; let me show you what despair really is like for a man like me! I am the only one of my kind. Nobody else is like me, so listen to me!"

The crowd remains silent for about eleven seconds; then they all simultaneously scream at the top of their lungs. They scream like they just witnessed a sign of the apocalypse; they scream with the loudest noise they can generate. They scream my name: "Zach! Zach! Zach! Zach!"

This is truly an unexpected response. I never thought I would see anything like this. I criticized my own writing; me—the man they adore. I insulted their intellect; I called them gullible. But yet, I made a crowd that sounds like animals turn into a crowd that sounds like possessed people. *Look at this*, I said to myself, *these people worship me*. These millions of people are part of an effect: one person says something, and millions of brains follow blindly. These people are awestruck dogs: you can beat them, love them, or instill fear in them, but they will always come back to you with reverence.

I will show these people how a guilty author writes; an author who faces agonizing emotions head on. They will read my autobiography. I drop the mic to floor, throw out a peace sign with my fingers, and walk off the stage into the tunnel. All I hear is, "Zach! Zach! Zach!"

In the tunnel, Manny stands. I walk up to him expecting an earful about how he is going to quit or how I disrespected him on that stage. Instead, he grabs my left arm and pulls me toward him in a strong hug. He hugs me with such powerful emotion that memories spring to life. I remember happiness and emotional security. I remember Mark's hugs, and my brother's and mother's hugs, and all those who have ever tried to show me that they love me. Manny reminds me how it feels to be cared about and loved, a feeling that I almost completely forget existed. I pull out of the hug, smile, and say, "Manny, truly, thank you for that."

He looks directly at me and says, "No, you are owed this. Don't thank me."

In this last thirty minutes, I have experienced brilliantly positive emotions. I have experienced happiness, emotional stability, and what it feels like to let something positive off my chest. Emotions like these are hard for me and I hope to God that they are not taken away soon like all other gratifying emotions I have experienced in the past. This juncture in time and emotions is a recipe for an earth-shatteringly successful book. All I want to do is write like the old days, write like I know no better than to pour my heart into it.

Look at those lines in the sky,
the memories flow back to me rapidly, as I came to
this empty bench just to lie down.
Wait, just listen to this story before you stop reading,
walk away, and say goodbye.

Those are the same lines I saw in my childhood; I feel like all I want to do is cry.

What if my destiny was daunted, and I was one of those people who lived for a short time, to just die?

Don't you think, I think about that repetitively?

Why was I chosen to have this life, why was such an amazing destiny chosen for me?

I was crafted so profoundly:

built as a prodigy.

So I thought,

before I was in the battles I have fought.

I wish I was taught,

as a young man, not

to search constantly for more.

I wish I was just your average bore,

who read the newspaper at the same time every Sunday.

I wish I regularly woke up every day and turned to my wife and kids and said,

"Good morning, honey and kids, how was your day?"

But damn, I am and always will be a social outcast.

As much as I have always found ease in fitting in, the comfort would never last.

And in no time, by my persistent brain, I would be harassed.

If I was given the opportunity, I would have passed.

But I wasn't; it just happened all too fast.

One minute all I wanted was just a little more than I had;

the next minute I was driven mad.

I was mad, but at least I had

on my head a crown,

and with that crown I could show all the people who ever hurt me that I was no clown.

And I could make them all frown,

because they would all realize their tragic mistake of fearing the gifted.

That even though I was just a kid,

I possessed the ability to ridicule them all.

That ability made me believe I was genuinely happy for a long time, until I abruptly realized I had been thrown into a deep hole.

A hole so deep and scary that it darkened my soul.

My saddest realization came when I realized toward the end that I was the greatest fool.

I was in the story, the pathetic mule.

Praised independence I did, but my need for satisfaction caused me to suffer under my own rule.

I don't expect that you'll

be able to understand it much, but these people I felt superior to, were always the real winners, even when I found success in my desire to ridicule

them all, in every direction.

Look at them now: with the people they love, they have an undying connection.

They can live with an imperfection.

They aren't so sick that they feel taunted;

they don't feel bothered by an imperfection, because they are not haunted by it.

With ease, they block out the unwanted

emotions, something I thought, before now, I could do.

I was wrong; now, with any attempt to do so, I appear cuckoo.

With little detail, I have now told my story to you.

My restlessness and sadness grew;

that is all you have ever knew.

But what if I told you that every story should have a happy ending?

That forever, man's heart will be lending.

That I won't always be myself defending.

And I will die happy without any pretending.
These rules of life were made for bending;
I will find for myself true happiness,
I will search for it until in my life, I find bliss
I won't continue to live everyday feeling this
same sadness.
I write here to tell you all,
that despite all my horror,
I won't end this chapter without discontent.
Even if all I have ever earned had to be spent;
I will allow my happiness to augment.
Never will I find anything again to resent!
My new destiny is to embark on this journey toward
contentment;
Just please pray that I find it possible in my life
presentment.
And know one more thing, every direction in which
I have went,
I have derived from it knowledge and experience.
For that will be my registry to genuine brilliance.
And by the way, since
I first started writing, this is the first story in my own
view.
So for those who did not catch on, don't wonder who.
Let us now open a new chapter.
And see for ourselves what has been to my recent
depression the real factor.

I write now in authentic, non-poetic voice. This
book is a description for you all to comprehend
a concept I have mastered throughout my years,
the concept of control. Control now lives to haunt
me, but it was not always like that, ladies and
gentlemen. It has truly given me every feeling or

emotion imaginable. Control made me superior to you all, and also inferior to all.

My previous stories were my views and beliefs disguised as fictional characters; so my request as you read this is not to panic as you enter a realm of the psychology of pure obsession and dissatisfaction.

In this book, my goal is to give you complete honesty. To be completely honest, I am not obligated to request that you do not flee from my book as you read it. I simply do not need to, because whether I ask you or not, you will read through the book, whether you want to or not. Your brain has subconsciously been ordained to want more of my words, if you have not noticed by now. I only ask you, because you should get the occasional luxury of being fed into your pride, as you did constantly to me. And, to clarify, I am not bequeathing to you my stature. This is merely a message from an exalted one to the servile individuals you are.

This story must start with my acknowledgment that I am potent in appearance, weak inside. I have wronged you all, and this is my attempt to repair what I have broken. If anybody had told me at any point before this that I would beg for your forgiveness and attempt to connect with you emotionally, I would slap him in the face and call him a storyteller. As I write this, I find myself hardly believing what I am currently doing. I am vulnerable because I betrayed you. I never knew betrayers could feel vulnerable after betrayal and achieving superiority. Yet my beliefs are often proven wrong. Finally, I would like to tell you my greatest personal issue: I don't believe this earth has generated a bigger, purer hypocrite than I am, and for that reason, I loathe myself.

Now that I have informed you about my deepest, darkest fears and reasons for my now grievous personality, I will begin my story.

My most spasmodic memory, which has recently leached into my happiness, is a phone call with my brother—the brother who got me knotted into this now futile mess called fame. We were talking and I, because of the pain of internalizing everything, had to externalize my feelings about my fame. I spent the night talking to him with composure, and he understood, until he naively asked me a question. He asked me about my biggest regret.

His question felt like a slap in the face, I realized something, which immediately filled my heart with a burning sensation. I realized that he was the man who inflicted this pain on me. He had brought me into this fiasco of fame. I responded extremely emotionally. I shouted at him through the phone, blaming him, shouting words that I never want to say again. I was impaired and needed to blame someone. I needed a method of relief. I made him listen to my shouts and angry phrases until I had no more to say.

The entire time, he stayed quiet and allowed me to express myself. This quietness showed me that, no matter the issue, this person puts my happiness above his own pride. When I finished shouting, I realized that I had been looking for someone to blame, because I was incapable of acknowledging my own wrongs. I asked Muaz what he had to say. He said I was absolutely right and that truly was his greatest regret. His docility shattered my insides. My heart cried, which had never happened to me before.

I cried over the phone then and told my brother—whom I needed more so I would have found myself on this path anyway—that it wasn't his fault. I tried to tell him that I was the one who wrote, not him. However, he would not accept it; he allowed me to be the victim while denied his own pride and values. He did not have to tell me this; the empathetic side of me understood this right away. Now, it had all changed, my entire view of my brother. I have always loved him, but now I revere him. I live to pay homage to him.

I tell about you this memory for three main reasons. First, I want to show you that, though he is unusual, my brother introduced me to a new type of love, a love greater than anything imaginable.

Second, I am no victim in this equation. I am the wrong one, I am the inflictor of pain. Whether it had been my brother or somebody else, my works still would have been recognized, and I would be in this same position today, because I have a pathetic inability to be satisfied with what I have. My brother was just the path I happened to take, but any path would have led me to the same destination.

The third reason is the most jaw-dropping reason of all: his reaction to my foul language. His reaction was nice, but it what truly shocked me was the feeling I felt afterward. It was a feeling of nostalgia, the rare feeling I had when I was a young boy and was learning the words of the Prophet in our religion and his means of communication. I was told that he was among the most noblest of men, and his demeanor proved it. My brother's reaction reminded me of the Prophet's reactions, which reminded me about religion. Once I felt the comfort of religion flow through my veins quickly, I also felt a warmth in my heart. For the first time in my life, I felt secure about religion. Then the feeling vanished again.

Since then I have obsessively tried to feel again what I felt that day. I have refrained from drugs and alcohol. I have refused to fornicate. And what I was too scared to announce to you all on stage is that I prayed to God. I prostrated before him. I prayed to God, yet I could not regain that feeling I felt on that day. I tried everything, and it has been so frustrating for me to not regain it. I searched for a method for o regaining it, to feel again what I felt in my heart. But I had no success until I stood on that stage two months ago, and a feeling penetrated my heart. I had figured out the method for renew the feeling. On stage, I knew what I needed to do, so I announced to you my depression, self-loathing, and more important, my hypocrisy. Suddenly, the guilt in my chest lessened slightly, and I knew why everything was the way it was.

I write this not to ask anything of you, but to narrate the pain of deprivation. Deprivation from love, from happiness, from comfort, from a smile, from security, and from anything positive. Before this book, I dealt with nine months of writer's block. I could not write, not even a damn sentence. I wanted to escape from life, and I could not do that either. So once I retained temporary happiness from religion, I snatched at the opportunity.

This book is called *Control* for several reasons; so many ideas and stories led me to choose this title. Control is the idea of determining the behavior of someone or supervising the running of something. I believe that human beings control our own fates. There is no written prophesy or predetermined destiny that regulates our actions. We are made to illustrate our own paths. We are given this majestic brain that has the ability to do so much, and it is our responsibility to the world to use it properly. The lazy, unsuccessful man is no different from the successful man in that they both have chosen their own paths in life.

All this talk about fate sounds like a cliché, but I bring it up not as some type of motivation, but to question what fate really is and to express the idea that humans do not have absolute control.

My life has been plagued with troubles that I could not control and that torched my heart. These troubles include my separation from my sisters and the suicide of Wyatt Kimmel. As much as I am scared to admit it, these troubles created the successful man I am today. The agony I felt when I underwent those harsh times reminded me that although I believed I was different, although I believed in my superiority over mankind, I could not control everything. The first few times I experienced what I could not handle, I got weak, like a handicapped hunter. I got so weak because I stumbled on my pride was life and its miraculous experiences.

Through the stronger side of my heart, I learned so much. Pain is a virtue if you see it as so.

The greater idea that I have recently mused about over days and nights has become the most powerful question of my life: *Why me?* This question seems heavier to me than any mountain or ocean on the planet. This question humiliates me and encourages me simultaneously, in a way that no other question has. Why was I chosen for this life? More than seven billion human beings walk this earth, and I was the one chosen to lead this high-profile life. Why me? Why was I sent to motivate and emotionally encourage others, to destroy others and cause them pain, to teach people about questioning reality and God in the heaven, to be seen as a "legendary philosopher" or "king of mind manipulation." Why me? More than seven billion people; how come no one else on the planet became what I have become.

This concept has to be more than choosing one's own destiny or writing one's own fate. Nobody can carve out a life like mine, and I say that with zero pride or boastfulness. I was given this brain, and I maximized its abilities. Why wasn't I a ten-year-old child run over by a car or somebody struck maliciously by cancer? Why have I lived this life while billions of others haven't? Why have I lived this life while millions of others are in their graves? Who am I?

The more I ask myself this question, the more the answer vanishes. I have no answer except that maybe I am the product of a supernatural figure, like God. Do I owe him thanks or prostration? I have no answers for these questions. I believe in him, but my merciless mind overtakes my mercy for the world and my love for him. To whom do I owe all of this? Whom should I praise for what I have been given?

———•—••—•——

I do not read my mail. I never do. I do not have the time or the desire to read mail from people. I am truly sorry that I've failed to acknowledge your attempts to reach me. However, one envelope that was blue as the sky caught my eye. It was lying down on the floor in my garage, with some other useless mail that was to be thrown away. I rarely enter this garage; the housekeeper has the job of throwing out the waste. However, for some unknown reason, I walked into the garage without apparent purpose. I scanned it quickly, seeing nothing appealing, until I laid my eyes on that blue envelope. I felt compelled by it. I bent over and picked it up. I walked out of the garage, got into the elevator, and went upstairs to my room, with the envelope in my hand.

I locked the door to my room, walked over to my black-coated bed, and lay down. I ripped open the blue envelope and pulled out the piece of paper inside. It bore a color picture of me holding a mic at a San Diego awards ceremony last year. Below this picture read: "By Connor Sanders. To the king, Zach Smith."

On the back were two paragraphs, followed by a farewell, as though Connor and I had met before. The note read:

> The history of life has witnessed this phenomenon countless times. Witnessed it has the determination of man, miracles,

stories, and etc. It is not naïve in any possible way. This life has seen everything before, some things more than others. One of the very rare things it has seen is a man called Zach Smith, who possesses the ability to kindle hearts of billions as well as befoul hearts. He is a man who possesses the ability to love as well as hate. He is a man who is both kind and evil, both dependent and independent. If his love and hate, his melancholy and happiness, were placed on a scale, they would be of equal weight. He is not materialistic like the bottom-dwellers of this world. He is supernatural, like a god.

He has found the formula to lead mankind, this man, Zach Smith. He found the formula through balance and aptness, through the three main components of leadership—punishment, reward, and storytelling. This man used these three components to teach the unteachable, love the unlovable, help the hostile, and create for this world an eye to ponder unlike ever pondered before. These components mastered by this man have only been seen in one other instance, i.e., in God. His abilities and esoteric brain activity lead to the inevitable question: is this brilliant philosopher really God disguised as a man?

Connor Sanders

I have known extremists among my admirers. Usually, I would throw a message like this to the side and dismiss it as unimportant. However, the power of this piece of paper really paralyzed me and left me flabbergasted. I was unable to dismiss it. I held it silently for fifteen straight minutes and then, finally, normal thoughts begun to reappear, or so I thought. I remembered the story my father used to tell me about two men who kept praising one man until he threw dirt into their faces, yelling at them for giving him a false belief of superiority. The people praising the man were actually harming him. Is the author of this note similar to these two men? Is this an attempt to supply me with a false belief of superiority? Or is he asking for true reason?

The reason this note stuck with me so much was the sequence of events that led up to it as well as the words he wrote. I never read notes but I somehow felt the aggressive urge to read this certain one; I took it up to my room and made certain I was aware as I should have. Then came the words, which were more than just praises; these words were different. They had a way of seeing through me, of understanding my demeanor. It was as if I had written this note. How could somebody understand me at this level? He introduced me to a part of my character that I had not realized I fore; he introduced me to my double personality. The words he said were correct; I have evil and kindness in the same in quantities. I am as generous and loving as I am a loather and distasteful. These were miraculous insights that I had not known about myself.

The second thing that he said that got to me was that I had mastered a balance between the three elements to true leadership— punishment, reward, and storytelling. Too much punishment produces fear and rebellion. Too much reward does not instill fear.

Because of storytelling, nobody will attempt new things because they already will know the result. It is brilliant to see the way this man inferred that I cultivate people using these elements. It is as if the note were written by an angel or a devil.

And his last question has stayed on my mind. Am I, the great philosopher, really a god? Am I God?

—◆—◆—◆—◆—

Ten months after the book …

I experience morbid disgust as the numbers are presented to me—morbid disgust where there once was a mesmerizing feeling of fulfillment. I sit in this dim-lit restaurant; all once loud noises around me are suppressed. I hear no external noises; all I hear is myself. I hear the sound of a hundred tea kennels whistling with rage. I hear screeches and hatred, voices that say, "You made it come to this. Now there is no way out." And one response comes to my mind: *True.*

It has been fifteen years since I writing, fifteen years spent angrily seeking revenge. I worked and believed in my cause like a martyr, and it took fifteen years to reach this final destination. A destination where I and everything I have ever done are hated. A destination that crosses paths with stupidity. A destination that knows that I am naïve and have spent my entire life chasing a cause nobody else gives a damn about. My whole life has been worthless, because in the final moments, I realize I do not have anyone to love in this artificial world—not a lover or a fan. There is nobody I can look at and say "I love you."

The old accountant keeps repeating, "Best-selling book series of all time" and "more than most religious books, more than any biography, and more than any friction book ever." If this old man even knew how much he was upsetting me, he would immediately stop. These numbers are wrong, morally wrong, and they insult me.

I conclude one of the worst meetings of my life, walk out of that pathetic and overrated restaurant, and walk toward my car. All I can think about are holes—the shapes of holes, big holes, small holes, deep holes, shallow holes, canyons, volcanoes. I envision myself in holes and the bigger they are, the more that I belong in them, unable to escape. People don't know this, but I am a digger. I can dig deep, human-swallowing holes. I have successfully dug the deepest, most treacherous hole—one that no man nor woman can leave. I have dug a hole for myself in which I am locked forever; I will never leave it. The books are my tools; evidently, they are better than shovels. They have locked me in this hole and deprived me of my freedom.

I am trapped in this hole with my monstrous self. Books, you certainly will be the reason for the end of my existence.

CHAPTER 9

I laugh sometimes, whenever I feel any form of anger. I laugh at the way she smiled when she told me that "anger is only ever driven by fear," and I laugh at the way I looked in her eyes. I still laugh at it today, even though it is nearly twenty years later. There is truth in her words. I am unable to find a falsehood in her statement. I forget your name, former friend, but thank you for the lasting advice.

Our minds are all about fundamental instincts. Several components help us sustain our sanity; without them we would be almost primitive or mentally unstable. The anger that I sometimes feel is solely my mind replacing my deliberate fear with something more ego-friendly. Think about it. Recall any anger you have felt, and you will realize that it springs from fear. This is true for even mild moments of anger, like when your brother leaves the house with car you were supposed to take to the doctor's office. That "anger" is your fear of the consequences or embarrassment of missing your appointment. What about days when you lash out angrily at everybody around you because you had a bad day; that is the fear that you might lose something or be forced to face difficult consequences.

Whatever we believe, there are fundamental rules that give us the optimistic ability to wake up in the morning, even through depression. Silly me for thinking that I could escape these fundamental rules. It was arrogance that made me even attempt to disregard the laws of humanity. Silly me for trying to dispose of my feelings of dependence, for attempting to channel them in a different direction

I tried to depend on my given intelligence to feel secure. I tried so hard. I tried to write as a way to fulfill my dependence. Everything I tried worked, but only for a little time, because as quickly as it rose, it miraculously declined. Now I understand why so many great artists go insane or become corrupt, like me. Intelligence will not take you far if you do not believe in anything. Believing in nothing except the idea of cultivation of human minds will result in a lack of contentment.

As I grow and mature, I realize that to be happy, you have to believe in something certain, something you love unconditionally, something you are willing to die for. And never replace that belief with a human being, no matter how close you are to that person, because man is weak and will fail you in times of despair. No matter who they are, they will fail you, whether purposely or accidentally, because they are people like you and me.

I have done so much wrong to this world but in particular, I did not keep my word. I wrote and stood on stages screaming unfathomable ideas to the world and then lived by a different set of ideas. Hypocrisy is the absolute worst wrong I have ever committed, a wrong I am unable to live with, that I have chosen not to live with because happiness is far from attainable.

I know in my heart that a man's word is his pride and the only thing that will hold weight when measuring who we are as people. And my word is flawed, so flawed that I have corrupted the minds of millions. A world like this will never give me happiness; instead, I will continue my disgusting tendency to self-loathe.

Farewell, to the atmosphere I know now, the atmosphere I o tragically created for myself and for millions upon millions of other people. I have tried to fix my wrongs, to replenish the minds of the people that I have destroyed, but there is no hope, because the damage that I have done to this world is irreparable.

Farewell, because my only other option is to flee; and flee I shall.

CHAPTER 10

There have been several reports, stories, and theories about the disappearance of Zachary Smith, the world-renowned writer. Did this man choose to run away from what he loves, or did the world rob him and kick him away from what he loves? As a result of Zach Smith's disappearance, the world is experiencing a colossal destruction of inner peace; men and women are growing restless. His disappearance is detrimental to all. The question that nags the men and women of planet Earth is: where is Zach Smith?

The only people who connect with Zach Smith during his nine-month-long disappearance are Sarah and Mia; or so we (the world) thought. After an in-depth interview that streamed live across the world, we realized that their knowledge of their own brother is limited. They know hardly anything. In fact, according to Sarah and Mia, he has alienated them for the past few years, which seems almost unbelievable.

This reality is hard for people to fathom and accept, because we know from Zach Smith's writings that Sarah and Mia played a crucial part in his well-being and his life.

Nine months, and he is nowhere to be found. Where is the great Zach Smith?

———◆—◆◆—◆◆—◆◆———

"He gave us everything we ever needed, in every way," says Mia to Mark Jacobs, the host of the TV show. "He supported us financially and emotionally. He called us and visited us in California often. For many years he was Sarah and my go-to source when we were in despair. Then he visibly started to decline. He grew tired of everything around him; he got sick. He started to believe he was crazy.

"About a year and a half ago, he told us that he would stop seeing us. He mailed a letter to Sarah and me, and I believe Muaz and the rest of his family got a letter too. Our letter basically said that he had become insane and he did not want to destroy us in the way he had been destroyed. He wrote that he cared about us so much that he wanted to keep the insane man he had become away from us, and that this would be temporary. He was deeply hurt but he wouldn't let us help him because he wanted to help himself. After that letter, he continued to send us money; he was very generous. But that letter was our final communication with him."

Jacobs turns to Mia's sister. "Sarah, tell us about your current relationship with Zach," he says.

"Well," says Sarah, "As Mia said, it ended with that letter; that was our last direct communication. We made several attempts to contact him, but he never replied. I even drove out to Los Angeles to visit him once, but I was denied access into his residence."

"Sarah, has this abrupt decline in your close relationship with Zach caused you to be angry with him?" asks Jacobs.

"Honestly, no, it has not," Sarah replies. "Mia and I have known Zach our whole lives, and if there is one thing we know about him, it is that he cares more about us than anyone else he knows. When he was in his teens, he used to feel immense guilt when he left us to go back to his mother in Oklahoma. Zach cares about us and no matter how hurt we are, we always know deep in our hearts that he's done everything because of his love for us. And you know what, this may seem odd, but I believe he speaks to us through his writing. He wrote about us often; even though he did not specifically use our names, we knew it. Zach cared about us so much. He is the greatest man I know, and I hope he is okay. Zach, if you are listening to this, we love you to death. You are the greatest writer we have ever seen. Please come back."

Sarah tries to hold back tears but she cannot. Before she knows it, she is bawling. Jacobs grabs a napkin and gives it to her. "Wipe your tears," he says. "Everything will be okay, hopefully." He pats her on the back to comfort her. Then he turns to the camera and says, "Well, this has been an exclusive interview with the half-sisters of Zach Smith. Goodnight, ladies and gentlemen." The curtains close as the audience in the room claps.

⋯•⚫◀◀⚫▶⚫•⋯

Everywhere—on the Internet; in newspapers, magazines, and posters—you can see tributes to the great Zach Smith. That he has been gone nine months without a trace is a thought that frightens millions of people across the world.

> Dear Zach Smith, end the mystery. Tell us where you are. Don't let our last memories be of you as a missing person.

> Dear Zach Smith, you are the world's inspiration. The world revolves around the brilliant artist that you are.

Please find your way back to us, because without you, the world will head into total despair.

We miss you, Zach. May the mystery of your disappearance be solved soon. End the despair that society must suffer without you!

CHAPTER 11

They say there is no worse punishment than death. How naïve they are. I know a punishment worse than death. I have lived it. It is the punishment of living as a famous man.

The night shuts the eyes of the normal man and opens wide the eyes of the fanatic. Our love for ourselves disrupts the flow of our sacred blood. The black crows of death become scared when they see an intelligent person turn insane. Insanity occurs when man attempts to love what he has created. Wisdom is the realization that man has not created anything; man is but an irrelevant grain of sand in the desert. Our brains become torched when we start to believe that we are superior. We are superior to nothing. Man's greatest enemy lies within his own skull.

Our creation is sustained upon one concept—that within our hearts lie seeds of dependence. Years of accomplishment only increased the severity of the obnoxious pain living inside me. My greatest fault was my attempt to manipulate the concept that keeps us alive within our own designated realms, which become broken barriers once man starts to believe in his own superiority. Self-loathing and melancholy disrupt our flow of existence as we search for a greater power within ourselves. I should have realized long ago that I was not special, that I was the same as every other man. I should have realized that all men are equal.

Unique to a truth, esoteric as a creation, special as a group member was the man I saw in my eyes. But the death of my spirit was the consequence of loving the one man I was not supposed to love.

———————◆◆◆◆———————

They'll never understand what it's like to be trapped in a cage with nothing but your passion. They think passion is great, but passion can never be great when it suffocates your spirits. People talk about the historic legends in this world as if their talent led them to their legendary status, but they are so wrong. A man becomes a legend the moment he realizes that his passion will kill him slowly if he fails to perform at that high level. Contrary to popular belief, it isn't talent that gets brilliant people where they want to be; it is their persistence. Everybody cannot be great. These people don't understand the pain I suffered. These people don't understand how much heart I put into each little word I wrote down. I bled the words I wrote. My passion was always to control the world, and not one person can say that I failed. The minds of all people were at my disposal, because I introduced ideas in a new style. I did what I the prophecy said I would do, and for that I will never feel guilty. I do feel guilty about the way I preached a message I came to disbelieve. I do feel guilty about telling people I hated the idea of loving something or someone.

The only people I ever loved were my mother, my brother Muaz, my sisters Sarah and Mia, and my childhood friend Albert. But my love for them always came with pain, as I questioned my feelings toward them. Do not misunderstand me. I love my mother to absolute death, but didn't she make me this way? Didn't she teach me that I am sick in the heart and the mind? It is her fault that I am this way, but as I grew I realized my foolishness would become apparent if I ignored how much she'd helped me. She helped me preach a message, i.e., that people should always notice what they tell a child, what they make a child believe and see. And I taught millions of mothers around the world never to make the mistake my mother made—by convincing her child that he was sick, so much so that it caused his madness. Because of her I taught mothers and fathers that they should never call a child a "damn, heartless narcissist." Maybe she ridiculed my mind as a sacrifice to teach the world how *not* to destroy a child, how *not* to create a cynical being. Maybe if the great God truly exists, as they say he does, this was his plan.

I will forever be thankful to my brother Muaz, but because of my sky-high pride, I may never tell him so. Still, I revere him in every way. Muaz, you introduced me through your brilliant business mind to this fame. And as much as I hate the devil that is fame, I will always love what you did for me.

Sarah and Mia are a different story. I love them so much that I believe I have surpassed love itself. I love them so much that their faces enchant me. But the question remains: did I help them and give them my all because of the guilt that lives inside me? Every time I talked to them I tasted my blood in my mouth, even as a child. They will never understand how much I loved and cared about them. Sarah and Mia, you are the reason I know how to love, but you will always be a question that lingers in my mind. And my greatest guilt is that I left you without a trace.

Albert, ironically, you are the character in my stories who symbolizes compassion. You were my first test subject when I was a young boy. I played games with your compassion; with you, I became the manipulative freak that I am. One of my worst mistakes was cutting you off when I decided that I wanted to singlehandedly control the world. I owe so much to you, and everything I am has to do with you. You are responsible for all the good in me.

Now, as I walk through these little dirt paths around my house in the Amazon rainforest in Brazil I see the undying love I have for these five people. I have escaped from the terrible world I lived in; people will never find me. Here in Brazil, I am just another young man living alone, someone I have always wanted to be. I am normal here, not the "prophet" I was in the United States and all over the world. "I am normal now." I say out loud with a big smile on my face, a smile so genuine that even I don't quite know how to comprehend it.

CHAPTER 12

Four years later …

I love her so much; it is crazy to think about it. Just the way she smiles and laughs makes me a better person. Her walk melts my heart. Just the mere thought of her makes me crazy. Her beauty scares me. Her sweet voice is greater than any music I have ever heard. She is so intelligent and articulate. It is as if she challenges the idea of love itself. I love her. I love Maria.

I love her so much, because she is my teacher; she is the woman who saved me. She saved me from the idea that I was incapable of loving anyone other than myself, that I was incapable of loving something without trying to destroy it. She taught me so much but her greatest lesson will come the moment she delivers our son and teaches me to be a compassionate father. The way I care about her feels unsafe, as if something ever happened to her, I would seize to exist. And I will make sure to protect my baby boy, protect him from myself.

I want to protect our son from the person I was and the person I can be. I will never allow him to know about the famous man I once was, because I am ashamed of what I was when I was on top of the world. My greatest fear is that Maria or my son will find out about my fame and the cynical man I was in my past life. For this reason, I live in the most isolated setting I can imagine.

I live deep in the Brazilian rainforest, with monkeys and all other types of wildlife. I spend much of my time marveling at the beauty of nature, which I never really loved until I came here. I never leave my property. I am always either in my house or sitting outside and enjoying the landscape. We get food and supplies from the closest city, which is about a forty-five-minute drive. Workers bring us everything we ever need. I keep my new family in our house at all times, because the thought of going out to the real world again scares me.

It scares me to encounter people again, because it was people I wanted to captivate and ruin. It was people who gave me those horrid thoughts of pain and hatred. The only people I stay around are my wife and son.

I hide from what I fear. I even stopped writing so that my wife and child would never see that person in me. From the outside looking in, the thought that I live my life as a huge secret sounds painful, but somehow it brings happiness to me. I feel unexposed and safe when trapped in isolation. I feel as though everything I ever was disappeared the moment I chose to conceal it.

Maria thinks my name is Joseph Smith. I told her that, because even four years after escaping fame I hear my name on the radio almost daily. All I hear are conspiracies and people's ideas about what happened to me. Everyone wants to know where I am, and she has heard so much about me on the radio and read so much about me on newspapers. Every time I hear her ask about the famous Zach Smith, I smile and say, "Maria, I don't know who he is really. I heard a little bit about him when I lived in America but never really cared enough to really know about him."

And she always replies, "How could you not know about him? The way they talk about him, it is as if he was like Albert Einstein or Jesus Christ." And being the curious and educated woman that she is, she tries to get her hand on some of my old works. Once she actually did.

I walked into the upstairs living room and found her lying on the couch reading one of my books. I panicked, ran over to her, snatched the book from her hands, and threw it at the wall. She looked at me with fear in her eyes and asked in her gentle voice, "Why do you have such a problem with me reading Zach Smith's books?"

And for the first time ever I yelled at her and said, "This man is a devil. He will make you mentally distraught. He will destroy your mind so quickly that you will not realize it. Don't ever read about him or anything he's written ever again! Where the hell did you even get that stupid book anyway?"

She looked at me, stood up, hugged me tightly, and said, "Joseph, do not worry, I will never read his works again. I just asked Andre, the delivery man, to get me a copy because they are flourishing all over the city even after his disappearance. I understand now. I love you, and if you'd like, it's only 9:00 p.m., so we could sit outside and burn the book in a bonfire together." Her passive response to my aggression was the greatest response she could have given in what was an emotional moment for me. For reasons like that, I love my wife, Maria. I looked her in the eyes with genuine contentment and say, "Yes, honey, let's burn that book."

I help her off the couch and walk with her to the elevator. We go downstairs and outside in the backyard. She sits down in a chair. I go back inside the house and grab the book and lighter fluid. I spray the lighter fluid all over the pieces of log and throw a match on it. As I am about to throw the book on the fire, Maria says, "Wait, Joseph, can I throw in the book since I am the one who got it? I am the one with a connection to the book, not you, right?"

She looks me straight in the eyes, and I shake inside. She stands up, gently takes the book from my hands, and tosses it right into the middle of the fire. Then she sits back down. "Joseph, sit down next to me please," she says. I am standing by the fire, still as a light pole. I sit down very slowly; it feels as if I am stuck in time. I stare at the fire and don't say a single word for about three minutes. Maria looks over at me and says, "Joseph, I know you well. I am your wife. You were really upset earlier, so I didn't ask you anything, I just comforted you. But you know I have a PhD in clinical psychology; at the very least, I can tell when I am being lied to, and I hate that you lied to me. You said you do not know much about Zach Smith and that he means nothing to you. If that is true, then why was your response to his book so emotional?"

I sit back and think very deeply about my response. For the first time ever, I feel challenged by this woman. She said she has a degree in clinical psychology and can spot a liar. I hate that she said that, because it is leaving me conflicted. It is making me see her as a stupid fool who did not comprehend what she just said, because my whole life with her has been a lie that she was too stupid to recognize. But as much as she just affected my view of her, I have to remember that I love her and the patient person that she naturally is. I have the choice of calmly telling her the truth and never lying to her again or making up a short story and manipulating her like I have done to others my entire life. I tell her, "Maria, honey, I did not necessarily lie. I never wanted to know who he was. I grew up hearing about him in the United States, and I have seen people be influenced by his potent words. I did not lie. I just wanted to protect you from his passive-aggressive words, because almost everybody around me became confused and distraught due to his horrible writings."

I chose to lie, because the fear that she will find out who I truly am is much greater than any satisfaction or relief I might feel by telling her the truth. And also, living a lie keeps my mind focused and gives the suspense that I have always craved.

Maria smiles at me and says, "Joseph, I completely understand, thank you. I am sorry for reacting the way I did." She clears her throat and speaks again, "But I have one question, and we will be finished with

Zach Smith. How can he be that bad when these are just short stories about men and women living a normal life and going through normal difficulties?" Her calmness reminds me how much I love her and that she is not just some idiotic girl that I can ridicule, like I used to do to other girls. She deserves a real answer.

"That is a great question, Maria. Let me answer it to the best of my ability. Though my knowledge about Zach Smith may be limited, I remember a line from one of his books. He wrote about a man who looks at his wife and asks, 'How can you worship a god who stole our child? Why would the great and fair God almighty do that to us?' When this author writes things like that, he discreetly teaches you to hate God himself. What is much worse is that even readers who did not adore God before reading the book change for the worse. When people doubt the fairness of a compassionate God, they doubt the fairness in all men and women and the world around them. The people who do worship God still believe in his existence, but they begin to despise him. Those who do not worship God begin to question and ridicule all of their surroundings. His books create tragedy and tyranny within the world and leave you to look to only one man as savior —Zach Smith himself. Everything he ever did was just a plan to gain control and reverence from the people on Earth. I saw people fall into his trap before I moved the rainforest. I was one of the lucky ones because I never read too much about him. I just knew of his effect on others. But I never cared for him, and I could say that a million times more. So, Maria, if you do love me and our child, please do not read his books or associate yourself with them ever again."

Maria sits there with her eyes glaring. She waits about a minute to speak and says, "Joseph, I see it all now. I understand everything. You are the most intelligent man I have ever met. Every time you talk in-depth like this, you leave me awestruck. Don't worry. I will not associate myself with the likes of Zach Smith again. He is a horrible man, the more I think about it, and props to you for seeing it in a way no other person could. I wish I knew how come you understand Zach Smith so well, especially since nobody else can."

I get up and kiss her right away, because she's supported me for the almost four years I have known her. I hope that one day I can tell her why I really do understand Zach Smith so damn well. I was the only one who did not fall into his trap, because I am Zach Smith, not some stupid irrelevant guy named Joseph. One day I will tell her my greatest secret.

I walk back into the house with my hand on Maria's belly, feeling the baby boy that she will bring to this world. I will raise him to become a better me. Maria is almost seven months pregnant, but I still cannot figure what to name him. I've thought about Noah, Muaz, John, but one name is stuck in my head: Zach Smith Jr.

For the first time in my entire life, I want to see a better version of myself, someone more noble and sweet, and certainly not a psychopath like me. I do not want my son to grow up the way I did; that way, he won't become the man I did. Everything I am is due to my poisonous upbringing, so surprisingly, I have no fear that Zach Smith Jr. will end up like me, because now I know what not to do. And I was always destined to become a great father. So maybe I will name him Zachariah Smith Jr. so that he can be a good man, which I never believed myself to be. I have always prided myself on how well I can read people by looking into their eyes. Before I choose his name I will look into his eyes and see if he really can become a kinder Zach Smith.

CHAPTER 13

Everything feels so surreal. I am standing in a hospital room as my wife gives birth to my son. It feels unusual to be in this situation, being the person that I am. I am in a Brazilian hospital, outside my house for one of the very few times since I met and married Maria. We live so far from the hospital; we drove thirty-five miles to get here. It scares me to be in this situation for the first time in my life. I feel so removed from my comfort zone. The only reason I can stand here without panicking is Maria—for her, I must be strong. I have to put aside my anxiety and fear about going out and being noticed. I have to be courageous—for her and for my son.

I hear her screams of pain while she delivers our son. I hold her hand tightly and say whatever words I can think of to comfort her. I reassure her that my love for her is limitless and that this baby will be the greatest thing that has ever happened to us. That I have always wanted to be a father and will be the best father I can possibly be. That I may not be experienced but I do know what not to do, because of everything that was done to me as a child. She screams in agony as the baby comes out and questions spiral through my mind. *How did I get into this situation? Will my life end in comfort and happiness? Do I deserve a beautiful wife and child? Do I even love her or am I fooling myself?*

I clench my jaw, hold her hand tightly, and try to enter a realm of mental peace as the baby comes out. For maybe the first time in my adult life, I ask God for help, specifically, in raising my boy. I whisper

Arabic verses under my breath, asking God to protect my baby boy. Protect him from the evil of this world and, even more, from the evil of myself as a father. As he comes out, the nurse grabs him right away and takes him into another room to clean him up. I stand quietly, a prisoner of the moment, until my wife calls at me, snapping me back into reality. "Joseph," she says.

"Yes?" I reply, walking over to her.

"We have a baby son; we have a child now. He came into this world. How do you feel?"

Man, that is a good question; how do I feel? Well, I feel scared beyond all recognition. I feel worried, undeserving, in turmoil. But I can't tell her that. I look in her eyes and say, "I feel at peace with myself and this world. I feel great." I kiss her on the forehead, and she looks up at me and says, "You look great. You look fearless. Thank you for being the strong man I always knew you were."

I am not sure that she is right, though; am I really a strong man? Maybe on the exterior, but inside, I feel rather delicate. I tell her, "I will never fail to be there for you when you need me. I will never let anything happen to you or our son." I wholeheartedly believe what I say. I believe that I, the world's most dangerous man, can protect my family from anything. However, my greatest fear is that I will be unable to protect them from myself.

While I am trapped by my thoughts, the nurse walks in with our baby boy. He is crying as loudly as he can. The nurse hands him over to Maria, who cries tears of joy as she looks at his face. He quiets down as we both hold him tightly. I realize just how much his face resembles mine. Now there is no way of turning back from my name selection. I want to name him Zachariah right now, and I have never felt so sure about anything. I take him from Maria's arms and say, "I want to name our son Zachariah."

She holds my hand and says, "Is that what you really want?"

I reply, "I am absolutely sure, I want to name him Zachariah after a man I once knew. A man who never failed to amaze me with his greatness. A man who always went by Zach."

"If that is what you want honey, then let us do it," Maria says. "But you do realize his name will be Zachariah Smith, as in Zach Smith, right? I thought you hated Zach Smith."

"Yes, I realize that, but I barely know anything about the other Zach Smith, and this one will a better version," I reply with enthusiasm. After everything I've just said, I feel like I've been slapped in the face. It is a wakeup call. Is this be the moment when I become honest with her and tell her who I really am? I mean, she will understand why I've lied if I explain everything to her. Should this be the moment that my life turns onto a whole new path? Much of me says yes, it should. But unfortunately, my fear overtakes all the other feelings I have and I elect not to confess. I do tell her what is perhaps my greatest secret. But I can't do this forever; I cannot be Joseph forever. I have to tell my family who I really am—just not today; I am not strong enough.

"This baby will be grow up to be a great and innocent man. I promise you that, Maria. I promise you that I will be the best parent I can be, and I will take care of you and Zachariah till death do us part."

"You do not have to tell me that, Joseph, I can feel it," Maria says. "I can feel in my heart just how much you actually care, and it is stupendous. I love you and always will." I kiss her and the baby. I pull a chair near the hospital bed and sit down. Everything feels so perfect. I am with my wife and my baby, indulging in one of the greatest moments of my life. A big smile appears on my face; it feels so pure. I don't think I could close my mouth and stop smiling if I wanted to. I have a family!

The doctor walks in and congratulates us on our new family member. He tells us we can take him home as soon as tomorrow morning. I can't wait to get him home. I miss home, my comfort zone. Maria and I look at each other and smile. I feel without fault for maybe the first time in my life.

———————◆◆◆◆◆————————

I hold Zach Jr. as we walk into the house for the first time in his life. He holds onto me, crying. I never thought I would say this, but the crying makes me feel safe. For the first time ever I feel protected by somebody other than myself.

I walk up the stairs, turning on all the lights along the way. I take him to our bedroom and show him the crib. The wooden crib is painted blue to signify his gender. I put him in it and stand beside him for about fifteen minutes until his crying stops and he falls asleep. I leave the room, turn off the lights, and close the door behind me. I walk into the kitchen and hug Maria. "How does it feel not to be pregnant?" I ask her with a sweet smile on my face.

"It feels great," she says. "I am going to have to get used to this again," and she kisses me. "Prepare yourself for endless hours of mothering and nurturing," I say.

"Joseph, you also should prepare yourself for endless hours of fathering and caregiving. We will both love being parents," Maria says with a wink. Then she adds, "Joseph, I forgot to tell you, we need to stay safe. When I was outside yesterday by the pool, I saw two different spiders. I wasn't sure how dangerous they were until I showed the doctor a picture I took of one of them." She pulls out her phone to show me the picture. "They are called Brazilian wandering spiders. Their bites can be fatal if they aren't treated quickly enough. We have to stay safe."

"I know about them," I tell her. "Don't worry. I will get somebody to get rid of them. I will protect you and Zach. Do not worry about anything." I hold her and whisper into her ear, "I love you Maria."

She whispers back, "I love you too. And I trust that you will protect us from the wandering spiders, right, honey?"

"Of course, I will," I say to my lovely wife, "Don't worry about wandering spiders at all."

CHAPTER 14

Is it okay to say I feel normal? Is it okay to say I don't feel like Zach Smith. I feel like Joseph. Am I allowed to say that I feel happiness and satisfaction like a normal person, perhaps for the first time in my entire life. Is Zach Smith allowed to say that he feels normal? It seems so peculiar and invalid coming out of my mouth. For the first time ever, things seem painless. And life is no longer moving in a downward spiral. I am not a mentally disabled man who fears everything anymore, I am a happy father in a healthy marriage with a superb wife. Constant thoughts don't haunt me at night anymore. I am free of worries. Maybe God has actually done me justice and cared for me. Maybe I was wrong all along about him the whole time.

I am not used to happy endings. I have built an entire career on unhappy endings. It is almost as if I didn't believe that happiness could exist after a lifetime of trauma. After a lifetime of chasing my "obsession," i.e., using people's minds as tools to reinforce my vanity, it feels nonexistent. My wife is the first person I have ever met who I do not see as a tool to feed my vanity.

It is so difficult to understand that these sorry tendencies have perished from my personality, that I have found somebody so perfect that she relieves me of my anxiety and my desire to trash people's minds. She is the person I have been looking for my entire life, my savior.

But I still have that dangerous mind that loves to pick apart each thought and feeling, I question what makes her so valuable in my eyes. What makes her so damn special? I sadly realize that I can't answer these questions clearly. I remind myself how smart and how caring she is and that she loves me to death; yet it seems like it is not enough. I cannot explain why this woman is so special that I was willing to change who I am for her. The world-famous Zachary Smith altered his perception of the world for her! And I don't know why.

I can think of only one reason, which is enough, at least for now, to sustain this long and loving relationship: perhaps I am not actually in love with the woman but with the idea of her. I am in love with the concept that I can calmed by the mere thought of her. Maybe my love for her is selfish; maybe I only use her to enter a sanctum of inner peace. But that idea is enough to make me love her. And I can never destroy the one person in my life who has ever given me happiness.

A marriage is a vow to stay together, side by side, through sickness and health; my vow is to stay with Maria through my own emotional sickness and health. I will stay with her no matter how damaged my mind becomes. I genuinely care about the woman who brought liveliness into me. As long as I am capable, I will stay with her. Hopefully, that will be for a very long time.

A family. I have a family. I have a happy family. We walk around the house and outside with such glee. Nobody ever seems unhappy. Everything is perfect.

The way she feeds him and nurtures him when he cries makes my heart melt with love and compassion. I don't think I have ever loved seeing something happen as much as I love seeing Maria care for our baby and raise him to be a good man. This family is the greatest display of happiness I have ever seen. And although he is young and this is my first experience in raising a child, I know exactly how to raise him to become normal and happy; that is all I want for my baby son. I want to keep him away from the evils I was forced to grow up with. I hated growing up with my family, but I thank them for raising me in such a terrible way that I now can notice any negative parenting styles and stop them right away.

I want my son to love me and to know that Maria and I will always be there for him. I still love my mother and father to death, and I started to writing to them and the rest of my family recently, for the first time since I moved to Brazil. But I never will forget the way they raised me to believe I was sick and incapable of happiness. I will never allow my son to see me as a man who ruined his love for life. I will always make damn sure that he knows that I will be there for him always. I will never ignore his existence the way I was ignored. Through the good, the bad, and the evil, I always will be Maria and Zach's main shoulder to cry on. I will be there for them physically and emotionally. My only goal in life is to love my family the way I was never loved, and cherish and care for them always. I will always keep them from harm's way.

CHAPTER 15

My heart pounds in my chest, which feels like it may explode. I run to the kitchen and call an ambulance. The few seconds that it takes someone to pick up the phone are the longest few seconds of my life. Once he answers, I immediately start yelling, "I need help, I need help! Do you speak English?"

"Yes sir, we do. What is your emergency, and where is your location?"

I provide my location as quickly as I can, as I feel my heart coming out of my chest. I have never been so afraid. "My emergency is that my wife is dying!" I shout into the phone.

"Sir, breathe; listen to me. You live far away from the closest ambulance stop. It will take us about forty-five minutes to get there and then forty-five minutes to get back. That is an hour and a half. The fastest way for you to get here is to put your wife in the car and drive here quickly. Do you have a car?"

"Yes, I do. We will leave for the hospital right now. Tell the cops that if they see a yellow Porsche 911 turbo speeding through the streets, leave it alone because it is an emergency." I end the call. My whole world feels in despair. I stuff my phone into my pocket and run outside into the backyard. I pick up Maria and run to the garage. I grab the keys and garage remote from the shelf and put her in the passenger seat; then I jump in the car. I press the button to open the garage but it does not work.

My body wants to sit there and panic, but my mind tries to fix the situation. I jump out the car as fast as I can and manually open the garage door. In frustration, I throw the garage remote onto the concrete floor, and it breaks into twenty pieces. I jump back into the car and drive. I start speeding the second I get off the dirt roads. As I drive, Maria stares at me and says, "I love you. It was not your fault. Do not blame yourself!" She says it passionately but quietly. A tear rolls down my face, and I wipe it off. I am unable to respond to her. I am traumatized. She continues speaking in the gentlest voice: "I love you Joseph, with all my heart. Please take care of Zachary. Be the great father I always knew you would be and tell him about me."

Now a face full of tears pour down my cheeks. "Maria, stop it. You will be okay. I am so sorry. We will fix this and everything will be back to normal." I feel my chest exploding inside and my heart crumbling to bits. I shake vigorously; every part of me hurts. "Babe, you will be just fine and we will both raise our son to be a great man together. I love you," I say stuttering with every line. My whole body feels painfully numb.

Maria looks up at me and slowly grabs my hand. She squeezes as tightly as she can, but I can feel her getting weaker. "Even when I am gone. I will always love you," she says, with a voice I have never heard come out of a human. She sounds like an angel.

"No!" I yell. "Stop saying that, my love; you will be fine. I won't let you die. I won't let you die. I won't let you die." The more I say it, the less I believe it. "We are almost there, Maria. Just stay with me, and I will save you."

Maria's voice is noticeably weaker. "Babe, Joseph, as much as I love you and I trust you with my entire life, I have to tell you that you can't save me. You are just a man; only God can save me. Pray to him, and ask him to save me. But I can feel him telling me that it is time to go."

The words stab me right in the chest. My body is dying slowly, just like hers. Maybe this is my chance to ask God for help, to pray to him and depend on him entirely for the first time in my life. "God, I believe in your every word. Dear God, please help me out of this dark spot! Please save Maria!" I say, shaking with anxiety. My spirit is being torn apart. "Maria, pray! Maria, help me get you through this." Now, I am asking her to pray.

"I am praying, Joseph." she says. "But I want you to promise me that you will take care of Zach and love him no matter what."

"Maria, I will. But we will do it together. You will be just fine. And it will never happen again," I am unable to accept the fact that she is on the brink of death. This could be the last moment I have with her ever, for the rest of my life. My mind won't process the idea; all I feel is denial. The car ride to the hospital is the longest thirty minutes of my entire life. But in fifteen more minutes, maybe even less given the speed at which I'm going, and we will at the hospital. Then we can take care of this issue.

As I drive on, my body shakes even more. My body is experiencing anxiety and terror. I try my hardest to get my mind off the fact that my wife could die any minute, but I can't. Tears stream down my face until they wet my lap. And every ten seconds she goes without talking, I get scared. I touch her and say her name until she says, "I love you more than anything" or "yes, love" or makes any damn noise to confirm she hasn't died.

The hospital parking lot is up ahead. I speed in and drive straight to emergency wing. I leave the car on and the keys in and grab Maria. I barge into the emergency room and scream, "My wife is dying! Help her now!" Nurses and doctors come running and take her from me. They put her on a stretcher and rush her into a room. I try to follow but they push me back softly, saying, "Sir, we need to help your wife. We will do our utmost best to save her life, sir. Please stay here for now."

I don't argue. I just go straight to the waiting room and sit by myself in a corner. I feel dead inside. I tremble in fear. I never cry, so it is like my eyes are watering so much to make up for the lack of tears throughout my life. My brain keeps failing to relay the message to my heart that Maria probably will die. Given the danger she is in, and how much time it took to drive here, it is highly unlikely that she will continue to live. But my heart refuses to accept it. How can Maria be dying? How can she die on me? How is this possible?

Two hours ago, she had been just fine, standing in the kitchen, cooking. Her beautiful smile radiated through the house, and everything was perfect. Everything. How could her life be ending? I sit there, struck by the moment, forgetting to breathe. Every thirty or forty seconds I gasp because my brain has forgotten how to breathe. Everything seems flawed. Life is pointless. I will never be able to mollify her pain; only one thing will fix the excruciating stinging in her body, and that is death. Death. The opposite of existence. Because of me, Maria will no longer exist on this planet.

I sit in that spot for what seems like forever, until the doctor comes out and walks right toward me. "Sir, may I have a word with you." he says. He stands tall, about six foot four, and his blue eyes look straight at me, as if to intimidate and blame me.

"Yes, what is the status of my wife? Please tell me she is okay!" I feel overwhelmed.

"Sir, I am so sorry to tell you that the venom destroyed her organs. She can no longer move. It is just a matter of time before her life ends. The anti-venom we gave her was not as effective as we hoped it would be. If you want to say any last words to your wife, this is the time, because we estimate that she will pass in less than two hours."

Tears cover my face, and I look down at the floor. Soon, the love of my life will be gone. My everything will be gone, and I will never be the same. I look at the doctor, and all I want to do is punch him in the face. All I want to do pin the staff inside this building and destroy it. But, for the first time in my life, I am too weak to do anything. I am too weak to even say a word. All I do is follow the doctor into the room and stare on the floor, without uttering a single word.

Maria lies down on the bed, staring up at the ceiling. I walk up to her and kiss her forehead as my chest tries to kill me from inside. "Thank you for being here for me," Maria says faintly.

"I ... I ... I am so sorry Maria. I told you I would protect you and Zach from wandering spiders but I did not. I am so sorry. I love you ..." I try to say more but the words won't come out of my mouth. All I can do is listen.

"You are not the wandering spider that bit me," Maria says. "You are the love of my life. You have never wronged me. Do not ever blame yourself for this, please. If you love me at all, do not blame yourself for this. This is life. At least you will be there for our son. You will always care for him. Please don't blame yourself." I stand quietly for about five minutes, but it feels like nine hours. The room is silent until Maria smiles and says, "Just promise me that you will kill the bastard spider that bit me." I giggle in an attempt to rob the room of its depressed spirits. But I cannot do more than a small giggle, because I've been torn apart.

It takes an hour and a half for her to die; it is the longest ninety minutes of my entire life. Depression flows through me. Every part of me wishes I was on that hospital bed instead of her. I watch her organs shut down, and then the doctors declare her time of death. I do not think I will ever be able to see a clock show 8:17 p.m. again without wanting to put a bullet in my brain. As I walk out the room in which my wife just died, they bring Zach to me and tell me to go home and get some rest. I hold him in my arms and hug him as tightly as his little body can handle.

I arrange for her body to be cremated, because a service is not the greatest idea for me. Watching my dead wife be buried in the ground would only increase the level of hatred and disgust flowing through my veins. Though I will never forget about her, the idea of cremating her body and getting rid of it quickly is the least painful method to me and the most effective at helping me move past the idea that she is gone.

I take my son to the car, and we drive back home. I don't say a word for thirty straight minutes. I am obsessed by the idea of death and the fact that it is happening again. When Wyatt Kimmel died, I died inside too, and I was never the same. It took me years to even somewhat recover from his suicide. Maria was much closer to me than Wyatt ever was, so her death will never leave my heart, especially because I know that it my own selfishness killed her.

It was my desire to escape the cages of fame and live a totally secluded life in the middle of the jungle. I placed us in the dangerous situation that got her killed. And when she brought up the Brazilian wandering spider to me, I told her I would protect her from it. I told her she had nothing to worry about. This time, my selfishness has killed somebody I loved, somebody I cherished. It was all my fault. And as I drive my son back home, all I want to do is lie down somewhere cozy next to him and dwell on the loss of my wife. But how can I lie down next to him knowing it is my fault his mom is dead. How can I raise my child knowing his mother's death is on my hands? The thoughts strike my brain like lightning striking a large body of water. The pain travels quickly throughout my body as I think about Zach Jr. and his future without his mother.

We get to the house, and I take him upstairs to the guest bedroom. I hold him tight and feel his tiny little heartbeats. He knows nothing about his mother's disappearance, but it is almost as if he does. He usually cries all the time, but in the two hours since she died, he has barely made a noise. He lies in the bed, just as quiet as I am, until both our bodies close down and we fall asleep. We asleep for the rest of the night.

—————◆◆◆◆◆—————

When I wake up, it feels like everything that happened yesterday was a terrible nightmare. But I quickly realize that it is true, which rips apart my insides. I sit up and look at my sleeping son. I reach over to rub his back, but all of a sudden, as my hand gets close to his body, I feel a sting all throughout my body. It terrorizes my insides. I cannot touch my son.

I lie back down and try to get close to him, but the closer I get to him, the sicker I get. I run right to the bathroom and throw up what it feels like everything in my body. I throw up like I have never thrown up before; my chest feels as if it has been smashed by a brick. My wife is gone and I cannot bear the pain—either physical or emotionally. My son hears me throwing up and starts to cry. I wash my face and mouth, walk back into the bedroom, and try to grab him. And then the cycle repeats; my body stings all over when I try to hold him. I cannot raise and take care of a son when I am the reason his mother is dead. Her last words telling me that I should not blame myself for her death play through my head. However, I cannot pretend that I was blameless. Guilt takes over my insides just like it did when I began to hate my fame. I do not believe I can handle this guilt.

I have to tell you: guilt is the most gruesome emotion a man can feel. It is the most possessive and destructive emotion I have ever felt. And the worst thing about guilt is that it one can never really escape it; there is no moment when you are free from the dread of guilt. Maybe if she'd just died, and it had not been my responsibility to save her from the Brazilian wandering spider, especially since I knew she had a venom allergy. Then, I would not feel so bad about her death. Maybe if it were just a regular death that was not caused by my secluded and dangerous lifestyle, the pain would not be so gruesome. Heartbreak and grief over loss is a feeling I can brush off, but fighting guilt has been my biggest battle.

I stand up and walk around the house; my chest feels grounded by an idea—that I was at fault. I walk around in pain until I go into my office, a room that I never use, and grab a notebook and paper. I have not written in years because of my fear that my wife would find out who I really was. However, writing is my refuge; it keeps me alive when I cannot live with myself. Writing is all I know.

Writing again may throw me back into that vicious cycle, but damn it, I know nothing else. I drown my pain in writing and then experience more pain because of the words I write down. And then I write more in a weak attempt to overcome that pain. It is a vicious cycle indeed, but at least this time I am not famous. This time, my writing will be only read by me, and it will not fulfill my dream of controlling and captivating people's minds. That is, not unless I slide right back into my old habits— chasing my vanity and feeling the need to release my writings to the public in an attempt to regain the control I once had. Hopefully, that will not happen; for now, all I know is that I am on the edge of depression again. And the only saviors I know are a pen, a piece of paper, and my words.

I sit in my office chair and start writing. I can hear my son crying upstairs; however, I do not believe I can help him out if I do not overcome this guilt. I begin writing, jotting down what first comes to mind.

> Never run, never hide
> Thoughts of poison dwell inside
> Leaving me mortified
> Guilt begins to reside
> Love is no longer applied
>
> You couldn't understand how much I loved the woman
> I killed

My biggest promise to her went unfilled
Now from sorrow, happiness I may never build
The truth is, fragmented is the way I believed I was
skilled.

Sick is my mind and heart
Penetrated by a loveless, noxious dart
Fate, my brain was never able to outsmart
Gone now from my arms is my sweetheart

I hope you never have to meet him
For his tyranny, there is no synonym
He will make all your pleasant sight grim
Leave all the bright lights in your life dim
To outduel him, the chance is very slim

He goes by the name guilt
Any direction you turn, his head will tilt
It is endless, the nightmare empire he has built
Your only wish will be that from the act of possession
of your insides he will jilt

I tear those words out of my notebook and throw them away. Is negativity the only thing I know how to write? Sometimes I truly feel that way. I am human, and so the moments of negativity and pain remain in my head much longer than the moments of positivity and happiness. Sometimes, as any man would, I get so caught up in the pain of something, I forget how the positive feels. My mind is much more affected by bad than by good; that may be the reason that whenever I do feel pain, it settles inside of me for a long time. Maybe letting go of writing infused with anger, in order to jot down sweeter feelings could become my true refuge to the blatant pain living inside of me. I start writing again on a new page, with a fresh mindset. I write about the way I felt about Maria.

Your eyes
Wipe away the lies
Drown out the cries
Until externally, my worry dies
Until out of this dark place I rise
And to the anger I say my goodbyes

Something about the way you smile captures me
If only you could see
To being content, you are my key
Everything regarded as painfully
To any such degree
Flies away beautifully

I do keep telling you about the release of pain
And maybe it's repetitively annoying
But I swear it's insane
To my blood you are the vain
To my corroded artery you are the brain
You are all of the sand as I am only the grain
To my disability you are my cane
To any loss you are my apparent gain
So surely you are the antidote to my pain

I am all but a habit
Of keeping everything inside, running away like a rabbit
But opened is this idea as I sit here and stab it
And let it flow in the air, made impossible to grab it

And I can't keep this inside
From this idea, I cannot hide
I have to tell you that I will always be on your side
And if you ever cried
I will also have cried

And if you ever disappeared, everything inside me
would have died
And about words like this I have never lied

I think you are beautiful
On the highest pedestal

My world is your world, welcome
my neurons, I have already sent 'em
In my mind there is a sanctum
You can feel everything now, nothing will be numb
Flavorful everything will feel, like Hubba Bubba gum
And as you walk through you will hear the loud drum

A drum I dedicated to your arrival
So don't worry about it being dull
You'll leave here with your heart and mind full
As you walk through an atmosphere known as lyrical

So to my heart, welcome by all means, as to you I write
Now you can feel how I feel when time is tight
And it's the middle of the night
But all I can think of is what I will write
And if you ever do see in this mind some light
And everything feels so right
Just know, I got that from you when in this relationship
we took flight
And flew high like a kite
Into my heart you took your deepest bite

So I owe it all to you, and I love you more than you know
You helped me grow
You lifted me from the low
If only how much I love you, you could know ...

My poem is about everything I felt about her, everything I always wanted to tell her. Afterward, I stare at it and cry, one of the few times I have ever cried in my adult life. Tears gush out of my eyes like a waterfall and spread all over the paper, smearing the ink. I cannot explain how I feel anymore; this is a feeling I have never experienced before. I am disappointed in myself, in my actions, by what I have become.

I, Zachary Smith, am the most destructive man alive today. Everything hits me at once; the questions slap me in the face. What am I? Who am I? The only answer I can think of is that I am a man who destroyed everything and everyone he and others have ever loved.

As I think about my life, I realize more and more that I did not just destroy everybody else's brain. I destroyed my own. Everything I have ever loved, I have killed. From the moment I began to find comfort in friends, especially my best friend, Albert, I kept them until I became tired of them and threw them away. I cut off a connection with someone who truly loved me as a brother and, as much as I hate to admit it, I loved him too. After destroying Albert and my many other friends, I began to love writing. Writing was my life. I slept ate, went to school, and talked to people thinking about writing. My entire life and everything I loved was centered around writing, and I destroyed that also. I destroyed it by running after my vanity and chasing my selfish beliefs and wishes, which were truly in nobody's best interests but mine. At least, that is what I thought at the time.

I cut off the few people I loved: my family. Though my intentions were good, I still came to the same end result. My intentions were to keep my family from harm's way by repelling them from the ruthless beast I was. I saw myself as grim. No matter how much I tried to convince myself that I was a person with a big heart and that I was the complete opposite of how I was depicted in my childhood—"a heartless narcissist"—the truth was that deep inside

203

I always believed what they said about me, that I had no heart. I tried so hard to convince the whole world that it was wrong in its perception of me, even going to extremes by trying to control the planet. I tried so hard to be a good person in the hope that I would one day be able to love myself again. But I never could. And I destroyed everything I did love.

After my family came the fame. I loved being celebrated by so many people after being scolded by a few people. However, the opinions of the few meant everything to me. I became too possessive of the fame until it started to kill me. I could no longer handle it, and I wanted to kill it. Everything I ever gain possession or control of, I drag down a mountain with me until I can no longer stand it. That's what I did with fame. And the most saddening aspect of it all is that the entire reason I left fame was because of the feeling of hypocrisy and because I wanted the feeling of fulfillment in religion. I left fame for those reasons, but I never followed through.

The most recent thing I destroyed was my love for Maria, my wife. I loved her with a fire, with a unique passion. All my life I manipulated and destroyed girls' hearts, never truly loving them. I spent my "love life" prior to Maria whispering sweet nothings into girls' ears, claiming that I loved them and so on. My entire love life was a mess and that was the biggest reason I loved Maria. She became the only woman I truly loved without wanting to destroy. She became the only woman I truly loved after believing that I was incapable of love. I loved her more than I ever loved anybody because she proved to me that Zach Smith is capable of love. And as much as I loved her, I destroyed her. She asked me to protect her from the dangerous spider and I promised her that I would, but immediately dismissed the idea. I dismissed an idea that resulted in a fatal mess. And like I always do, I destroyed what I loved.

I can never go back to the things that I have done; my terrible actions will forever be cemented in the history books of life. The last thing I love remains by my side; however I do not even know if I can raise and care for him. Will I have to give him up to free him from the brutal beast that lives inside of me? Raising him seems impossible at this point as the guilt clogs up the vessels of love that barely flow through my heart. I cry like I never have before. I cry out of pure disappointment in myself, my actions, and my way of life. I have never felt disappointed in myself the way I do now. Everything coming back to me genuinely reflects how incapable I am at loving myself. And it really makes me question if I will ever love myself, after hating myself for so long. And if there is no way to return a feeling of happiness to my heart, how will I raise a son? How will I love and care for him when I cannot even love myself?

I silently sit for thirty more minutes, dreading each moment of my life that goes by. I think about ways to fix my past, so that I can look back when I am an old man and find even an ounce of satisfaction in the life I lived. The way I am living right now, the path I have followed for so long only increases the likelihood that I will destroy more of what I love. And that is the last straw, the point when I realize that I need to fix what I have broken.

My mind presents me with the first step toward solution to my problems, one that will hopefully banish this depression from around me, allow me to get up from the desk and stop crying, and most important raise a sun to be great man. I stand up, walk out of my office and into the living room, and grab my cell phone. I dial some digits that I haven't dialed in years; somehow I still remember them. I call my mother. This is the first step toward self-improvement. This is what I have to do to be able smile again, a feat that seems impossible at this point. I call the woman who I have always seen as the reason for all of my problems because she told me I was "a heartless narcissist." This time, however, I'll put all my anger aside, and compassion will be the only emotion I choose to entertain.

I hold the phone to my ear and hear a few rings, until finally I hear a hello in my mother's voice.

"Hello? Who is this?" she asks.

"Mom, it is me Zachary, your son. I know it has been a while, but let's talk."

CHAPTER 16

She uses the exact same term she always used to explain my worst habit. She says, "I hate that you bottle everything up."

My mother tells me this as I lay my heart in front of her and let all the information I have kept hidden deep inside me for so many years seep out. I tell her everything, my whole life story. I tell her that she has always been right, that "bottling everything up" truly is painful. I let down my guard for her in a way that I never have for anybody else and lie down, embracing her mercy. Through everything, my mother is still my mother, and she understands me in a manner that nobody else ever has or will. I just wish I had thought of her this way so many years ago.

I stay on the phone with my mother for about three hours. I say that telling her everything is like slitting my wrist and watching the blood pour out because it is painful to expose my feelings to her like that. To everything I tell my mother, she responds with deep compassion. She tells me that I may be a grown man with an entire life of experiences, but at heart, I am just a kid searching for happiness. After I tell her that I wanted to be famous because I wanted to be admired and loved after years of being told that I was an evil kid, she apologizes for everything she ever told me. She tells me that she always knew I would be an influential figure in this world and that I was very intelligent, so all the everything she told me about my "narcissism" was to defuse my arrogance before it ever happened. She says that her greatest regret is the way she handled me when I was a kid, because she drove me to madness, searching for someone to admire me. She cries on the phone and instead of putting me down for the person I became, she congratulates me.

"I knew from day one that you would be somebody influential in this world, but I never expected you to conquer the earth. You may have written some words that were deep-rooted with evil, but Zach, you also changed the world for the better. Do not put yourself down for who you became, because you made such a positive impact on this world. You changed even my perception about it. You made me happier and more fulfilled; now I can feel sheer happiness because you taught me to see the world the way you do. You made millions of people happier by helping them invest in their creativity. Please do not put yourself down for the bad you did, because the good heavily outweighs the bad. I used to read your books and cry, and I still do. I cried so much, because I could feel your pain as I read your words. I raised you that way. For all the negative feelings you ever felt, I want to apologize from the bottom of my heart. I was wrong. It was my fault for hurting you so much. When you were growing up, I could never taste the pain you underwent, because you never knew how to express it. All I focused on was modifying you so you would not become a bad human being. I now know how painful it is to keep pain inside. My biggest regret was not knowing your pain." She tells me all of this, panting as she cries.

I agree to fly her, Sarah, Mia, and Muaz to Brazil as quickly as possible to come see me and reconcile with me. After telling her about my trouble in raising my son and my fear that I will not be able to raise him anymore, she reassures me and tells me that she will teach me how to raise him and love him unconditionally. She will help me as much as she can. She also tells me that she has another great regret, which she will tell me when she sees me. I call all my siblings, and they all agree to come to Brazil in three days

---

The moment is hard to swallow. I am, for the first time in years, standing in front of my family again. I remember how we were before. Sarah and Mia never lived with us, but having them around makes our family feel united as one. We spend a long hugging and harmonizing. I introduce my family to Zachary Jr. We sit in the living room and talk about everything we've never talked about before.

The scene is very calm. Our conversations lack intensity and emotion until I get up to pour some tea for my family. My mother looks at me and says, "I have to tell you Zach, my other biggest regret was not helping you build a relationship with God. Lately, I have gotten close to God and religion; it has truly given me a soft inner peace that I wish I'd had so many years ago. I raised you not to depend on God, and that was a grave mistake on my end. Because as much as we might not want to admit it, we have been searching for God this entire time. Zach, think about it. All the writing you depended on, the intelligence you thought you could depend on, the people you thought you could depend on, like Maria; they were all a search for something to depend on—God. I should have helped you believe in him long ago, because it would have helped you create a much easier path for yourself in life."

I gently put my cup of tea down and sit. I stare into my mother's eyes from eight feet away and do not say a word. I am speechless; never did I think I would hear my mother talk about how good God is or about how my path would have been different if I'd learned to pray. She continues to explain her point, and the more she does, the more it makes perfect sense. I have been searching for God this entire time.

"Mom, your point is a valid one," I reply. "Maybe I have been looking for an equivalent for the feeling of fulfillment that God instills into our minds. Maybe my mistake was finding somebody or something to depend here on earth and not looking in my heart for God. I always knew he existed, but I guess I never loved him or depended on him. But mom, I've spent so much time trying to ridicule God, scoffing at his idea of mercy. Loving God like you do is not something I am sure I can ever do. Mom, please, can we not talk about this anymore at the moment; it is too overwhelming. There is too much to process right now, I need time to think about all of this."

I smile and act happy as I hold my son in my lap. I am finally able to hold him again after feeling dreadfulness for days. The rest of the night passes peacefully as we all talk and reconcile. Genuinely, I can say this night is one of the merriest moments of my life.

We all wake up the next morning and make breakfast as a family. We make waffles and eggs together as we start the morning off with feelings of unity and glee. There is a feeling of genuine harmony as we cook and eat and laugh together as a family. Up until a certain point, our conversations remain lighthearted and friendly; we appear to understand each other, and conflict seems unlikely. Then Muaz makes a seemingly innocent remark, triggering a storm of anger that I was not aware I had. He talks about his life in the United States; he talks about how great and civilized it is right now. He talks about the adventures we had growing up as children. He refers to life in the United States as being the only adequate form of civilized life for me and my son.

He asks, "Zach, are you coming back to America?"

I say, "I cannot ever go back there, Muaz. You do not understand. I feel lifeless over there." It takes meticulous effort to be kind and patient as I explain my reasons for not returning to the United States. But Muaz cuts me off with another question that triggers my anger.

He says, "Your wife has died, and now you live here alone with your baby son. When will you return to civilized life, where you're supposed to live, back in America? When will you stop isolating yourself for no reason and being weird about your emotions?"

I take a long pause because every part of me knows that my response will not be pleasant. I look him across the table, straight into the eyes and, using gentle language, I tell him, "Muaz, I ran away from fame, from a terror so ugly it would rob any man of his ability to sleep. It would rob any man of his ability to smile."

He looks at me incredulously. Rather than saying an empathetic comment, he says something I interpret as ill-mannered. He says, "You exaggerate this hatred for fame, and you know it! You know that you had the money, the girls, the lifestyle, everything. Truth is, you left fame, because you're just overdramatic and demand attention all the time. Fame is actually nothing too big to handle."

My legs shake as I attempt to contain myself; however, my attempts fall short. I feel Muaz's defiance in his little smirk. Trying to remain sane only goes so far, as my insanity defeats me. I get up and throw the chair against the kitchen counter with a force that would make the NFL proud. I see the fear, the shock in my family's eyes. I want to sit down, breathe, and calm down. Unfortunately, I am passed that point. All hell breaks loose when I open my mouth. For the first time in my life, I do not think about a single word before I say it. I say everything lying on the surface of my pained heart. I blame Muaz for everything.

"I do not exaggerate anything. You wouldn't know because you were never me. You never accomplished anything worth looking at. You weren't one of the best-known men on planet Earth! You were not me. You have a cognitive inability to see what I go through because all of your brains are too small to understand anything. Do not sit here in my house and tell me that everything I feel is exaggerated! I lived and still live through hell. And it was all your fault. You brought me into this. I hate you. I hope you die. I stopped communicating with you for a reason. You are so goddamn dumb, and the saddest part is that you have more pride than I ever had, and I am your superior counterpart. You can live in this stupid world of yours thinking that everything is okay, but it is not! You ruined my life, everything I've gone through started with you. You brought me into this fame, and once in, there was no escape."

As I say this, I am slowly approaching him. I expect him to feel intimidated and keep quiet, but his mind doesn't change, and he says the same hurtful things.

"No, your fame was fine," says Muaz. "You had no reason to run from it. And maybe I didn't achieve the fame you did, but I promise to God that I am and have always been more successful than you. Because I am not sick in the brain like you are!" Muaz he walks toward me. The background noise of my sisters, mother, and my child screaming fade from in my ears. All I can hear is anger.

"I am sick? If so, it is because of you and your goddamn mother. I was always kind, and my potential to be a good man was through the roof. But you two had to convince me that I was sick! You told me I was incapable, goddamn you! I am the single, most intelligent man on Earth; right now that has been recognized. Nobody can do what I do with a paper and a pencil; no human has awareness on my level. No other human is like me, and that could have been a good thing, but you made me so angry, you ruined my life and the lives of millions of others in the process. I never bring this up because I don't want to hurt your delicate little feelings, but just know it was your fault." I am scolding him.

He looks at me and asks one question, in the most belittling tone I've ever heard: "Okay, Zach, please tell me why I am the reason you are sick in the brain. How is this my fault?" He has a little smirk on his face, trying to embarrass me.

I take a deep breath, blink several times, then walk up to him and shove him across the kitchen floor. He falls on his bottom but jumps back up and says, "See you're crazy!" I look back at my mother before I do anything, and the look in her eyes reminds me of my childhood—how I revered her and worked tirelessly to gain her love but was robbed of it. She looks at me as if I am truly crazy, and I stop for a second. But only a second, because although nearly every part of me wants to sit down and relax—I am a very docile person by nature—a more powerful part of me is the anger I have never been able to release the right way. I turn back toward Muaz and quickly walk toward him. He backs up. His eyes show a defiance that makes me respond to with violence. I grab his neck and push him against a wall; I hold his life in my hands. My family tries to stop me but they are weaker physically than I am and can't actually do anything. I hold his neck against the wall and see his face get red as I choke him. I loosen my grip a little so that every word I say will be heard clearly.

"I hope the guilt of what you did to me eats you alive. I hope you can't sleep and you dream about it. I hope you scream about it. I hope it haunts you until all your limited abilities are impaired. You are a devil; this is all your fault. You made sure I would get more and more famous for your own selfish reasons. Had you not been there, none of this bullshit would have happened. Let me tell you something you and I always knew, but my heart was too kind to tell you. And that is, Muaz, you will never be me; you will always be weak and solemn and stupid. I outdid you in every way. You will always be less than your younger brother."

I let go of him. He looks me in the eyes with a look I don't know how to interpret. It could be insubordination, but could be empathy. We just stand there, staring at each other as time seems to freeze. All the anger in me evaporates. Suddenly, I break into tears. I cry so hard that I can't breathe. Immediately, Muaz grabs me and hugs me, lifting me up as I fall on the floor. With a gentle tone, he asks me, "Would you like to go upstairs and talk, Zach? Just the two of us? I am not a bad person. I understand your pain. I was so wrong to say what I said. Let's talk about this, please."

"Of course, let's talk," I say.

He grabs my arm and directs me upstairs. So many things circulate through my mind as I walk with him. Memories of our childhood, memories of the times he screamed at me so I would feel his pain. He yearned for a heart to love his entire being; I never gave him that. But I could not give him that; all I wanted was to feel fulfilled. I could not see anything but my desire to live life at the top, to build an empire of my own, to fulfill my duty to this world as a brilliant mind. My heart was too dark to ever love him the way I was supposed to. I lived my whole life believing it was okay to disregard his existence. Now the guilt of it is catching up, all these years later.

We enter the upstairs guestroom; Muaz shuts the door behind us. We sit on the brown two-person recliner. We sit in silence for minutes until I ask him, "Have you ever noticed that I've had a brown recliner in every house I've lived?"

"Yeah, I have. Why?"

"Growing up I used to see the brown recliner in my room as my escape route. Every time we fought, every time Mama yelled at me, every time I got depressed, I would lie in my brown recliner with a notebook in my hand. I'd write about all the pain in my life. Muaz, I am telling you this, because I want you to understand. I lived through hell. I wanted to kill all of you, by being godly compared to you all. And that truly did happen, I did become a god in my own right. But a god is a god because of his failure to make mistakes. I made mistakes, grave mistakes. I forsook you. Maybe your desire to make me famous was you just trying to connect with me, when all I ever wanted was to be so damn far away from you. I can't lie. I wanted nothing to do with you. I hated you for making me feel this way all the time, but in actuality, I made myself feel this way. I was the reason I never felt complete."

"Zach, I love you, man" Muaz says. "Truly understanding something is through perception not as much with words. I want you to know that I understand everything—your pain, your hatred for the family, and your differences with me. And we will fix this. From now on, we will not be the same separated siblings we once were. We were born brothers and will always be brothers. Now give me the tightest hug, and this is to a new start."

I get up and hug him tightly. As I let go, I tell him, "I feel broken. I feel helpless." He grabs me and hugs me tighter. Muaz then says, "Let's go back downstairs and say hi to your mother and sisters."

It has been a week since my family left back to the States, a week that has passed more slowly than almost any other week in my life. I spent this week without sleep; instead I was filled with thoughts. Now I can hold my son and love him. My mother spent three weeks here showing me how to overcome the great loss of my wife ad to find happiness again. I am now able to hold baby Zach, look him in the eyes, and raise him to be the best man he can become.

CHAPTER 17

It's been fifteen years. Zach Jr. still does not know the truth about his father. I can't bring myself to tell him. What would he think about me, especially after all these years of saying nothing. What if he hates me? These have been the happiest years of my life, especially since Maria's death. I can't lose him too. Maybe he already knows. I thought Brazil was far enough away, but what if he learned the truth before he came here? What if someone told him, or he saw a headline about me? Maybe he saw my picture somewhere on the Internet or on the cover of a magazine. I feel unbelievable guilt; my son is all I have, yet I can't tell him the truth.

At times I feel manic, unable to go on because of my crippling regret. My conning days are long over. However, I can't shake the feeling that these things will catch up with me one day, come back to haunt me and pull me down with them. The nefarious deeds I committed on a daily basis grip me to my core and stretch me out like a torture rack. My sins bubble up inside of me as if I were an overflowing beaker; how can I go on? Where do I go? I feel like I've committed a murder. I'm constantly trying to string together conversations with my son, and the things he says to see if he knows the truth. Every abnormal statement is like a dagger in my side, throbbing to no end. I feel constantly on the edge, ready to snap. I know my health is worsening more and more. I can't keep this up; every year, I become more and more afraid. As he gets older, I feel as though he is dropping hints that he knows, and that my secret was never truly a secret at all. I feel a great urge to simply bring it up. However, I know my lips won't move even if my heart wants to get rid of this massive weight.

Sometimes I forget who I am, the lines between myself and my con-man persona continue to blur. My old habits slowly work their way back into my life, no matter how hard I push against them. I feel like my persona of Joseph was never supposed to exist; perhaps I wasn't meant to exist, even in my true form. Being a con man isn't my true nature; that's more clear to me than ever. Perhaps that's what pushed me into becoming the image-obsessed, narcissist I was. I was never meant to be so sick. I've made so many mistakes in my life. One blunder after the next; mistakes seem to follow me everywhere I go. The two best decisions I ever made were family related. Marrying Maria made me the happiest and the saddest I've ever been. I still struggle with her death; I can't believe she's gone. It crushes me to the core. She was always the only thing that gave me joy. But she was ripped away from me, which nearly drove me to madness; suicide sometimes crossed my mind. However, Zach Jr. kept me tethered, although even he doesn't know the true me. My whole life has been a lie, a string of dishonesty connected by vindictive actions.

I feel more and more that perhaps my mental health isn't the only thing that's deteriorating. I get incredibly strong, horrifyingly painful migraines; my head feels like it's being stabbed by thousands of hot needles. What's happening to me? Could it be that my symptoms are purely because my insanity is taking over and the immense stress of my guilt is weighing down on me? Often I am incredibly confused, dizzy, with blurred vision. My eyes almost stop working; they seem to be covered by fuzz. I need to go to a doctor very soon. Perhaps I'm dying. I can't leave this earth yet, not before I tell Zach Jr. the truth, not before I finally make amends for the lies I've kept secret for so long and the lives I tore apart. But how can I? How do you tell someone that you've been lying to him for his entire life, about everything, about the very basis of his existence. Where do I start? Where do I finish? Everything seems much more complicated, and yet the answer becomes clearer every day. The truth has to come out; it's no longer a secret I can hold onto. I wish I could just let it out; maybe that would help my health. I need to see a doctor before it's too late.

I'm going to call the doctor right now. I can't let Zach Jr. know anything is wrong. He doesn't need to worry and snoop around; that wouldn't do well for my situation. Picking up my phone, I realize I have a missed call. I immediately call the number; it's my doctor's office. I had an MRI not long ago to find the cause of my headaches; the results should be in by now. I am nervous about what I may hear.

The woman on the other end of the phone says to me, "Mr. Smith, we've been awaiting your call, and unfortunately we have some bad news." I immediately recoil in fear, knowing that many of my symptoms could point to something very serious.

I reply to the woman with a somewhat angry tone. "What's the problem? Am I okay?"

The woman sighs and says, "You might want to come in for this, just to run some more tests to make sure, before you get scared."

"Do I have a reason to be scared?" I hastily cry out.

"Not just yet, but we want you to come in just to make sure nothing's wrong." This woman has been assigned with the sad task of reassuring me.

"Okay, I'll come in, but can you tell me what you think the problem is?"

I can hear the woman's breathing become more labored, even through the phone. Perhaps I have put her in a situation she hoped she would never find herself. "We think you may have a tumor in your brain, but we can't be too sure yet, so please come in as soon as you possibly can."

I hang up without much more of a fuss. I begin to sweat, and my heart beats faster and faster. Then I try to reassure myself that nothing could be wrong. However, the feeling in the bottom of my stomach remains, sticking me harshly and strongly. Nausea nearly overwhelms me; however I muster up whatever strength I have left in my sick body and mind and force the feeling down. I run to the car, knowing that if I have a tumor, minutes, even seconds count. Possibly these are the moments that will decide my life. I race down to the doctor's office, and take the tests. I notice the doctor's mood changes after each test; have her suspicions been confirmed, or is she just having a bad day? Finally after what felt like an eternity, it is time to get the news, the information about my fate, and how my life will play out.

I command the doctor, "Please just tell me, am I going to live or not?" The doctor replies brusquely, "Unfortunately, it seems you're very far into the process, between a stage 3 and a stage 4 tumor." I sweat profusely; my heart pumps faster and faster.

I nearly yell "How much longer do I have?" as my fists grasp the arms of the chair. My patience wears thinner and thinner; I am heading back toward my old impatience, anger, and arrogance.

The doctor finally breaks down and tells me, "Days most likely; at the most a few weeks. Your cell growth is unstoppable; your tumors are growing and spreading at nearly unheard of rates. Your cells look absolutely unlike a normal cell."

How could this happen to me? How could I rise so high and fall so far—to die in such an absolutely miserable way? My demise will be swift, unstoppable, and pathetic. I look back at the doctor with a nearly indescribable expression of indifference. I slowly mouth "Thank you doctor, I'll be going now." I get up and walk through the door and the lobby of the office. I step into my car, look at myself in the mirror, and scream in rage, smashing my fist on the steering wheel. Nothing means anything anymore. I am going to die; I am fading away. However, I can't tell Zach Jr. the truth. I can't die without telling him. I can't just move on, and let him find the truth himself one day. What would he think of me?

Either way, I am dying. I can't afford to sit here and ponder. I don't have time to be selfish. The guilt is crushing me, but won't the consequences of the reveal be even more damaging? I sit in my car, filled with rage, sadness, confusion, disgust. The pressure on me makes my head ache; maybe dying will be easier. The symptoms seem to get stronger now that I know what is wrong with me. Maybe the stress of my impending absence from the universe is making me feel worse as is the stress associated with every other problem in my life. They all suddenly seem to have come to a head at one time. I wonder if I would be fine if Maria were still alive? Would my sick psyche have healed itself with her love?

It is hard to tell what turns I took to end up where I am now. What could I have done differently to keep Maria alive? Could I have done something so I wouldn't be diagnosed with cancer, or at least push it back a few more years? Even then, I'd just be stalling the inevitable reveal of my sickening past to my son. Maybe death will allow me to escape my responsibilities. In times like this, I find myself wishing that I had a god to turn to or a higher power to confide in, a partner in crime to push me to the right side. But I have no one to whom I can tell the truth. My emotions stir inside me; pressure builds. I forget if I ever believed in a god or if I just lied to myself, as I've lied so many times before. Regardless, my time is short. I don't have time to sit and wax poetic or ponder my options for fifteen more years. Decisions must be made.

CHAPTER 18

I woke up today, the day after my diagnosis, with a feeling of regret and pain in my heart. I dreamed about God, my mistakes, all of my sins—my defiance, my arrogance toward God. Yet God is so merciful, he has allowed me to see my son again, despite all the mistakes I made and everything I put him through. I was still too blind to see that the answer was in front of me the entire time. I've chased money my entire life; sickeningly, I've never given a penny away. While people starve and die of diseases that could be stopped with vaccinations, I sit on my golden throne, hoarding my money, which does nothing for me. I look at the numbers in my bank account; all those zeroes mean nothing. They sicken me now. It stirs hatred in my heart to know the way those zeroes were accumulated, to remember every sick decision I ever made, giving value to the dollar. I conned the less fortunate even after my bank account was already quite full. The book, did this; my fame, my obsessions. I hated humans and loved money; I lusted and had an absolute fetish for the dollar. Now, my money does nothing but mock me about my past. All my life has been wasted with greed, a deadly sin of which I've been guilty many times. Can God forgive me for everything I've done, all the horrible things—the scams, the greed? I denied him at every turn. Does such a benevolent being exist—someone so pure that he bears no grudge and harbors neither revenge nor desire to punish.

Apparently, God forgives all, but can that really be true? Are even sins as great as mine forgivable? My regret, and my heartache even if God were to forgive me, is that I am not sure I can ever truly forgive myself? Forgiveness is all I should be searching for, but it means nothing if I can't allow myself to move on from the past, and all the mistakes I've made. I think my fortune would do more good for the millions of people who don't know where their next meals will come from and those who don't have everything they could ever want. I'm going to do it. I'm going to give away all my money.

Or maybe I can't. I want to, but I wouldn't know where to start or which charities deserve my fortune. What does God want from me? Did he bring me down this road just so I could donate my fortune to the needy. Everything I've ever done … did he have a plan for me this entire time? I look longingly at my computer. I need to donate every last cent. I type my bank information on the keyboard with unbelievable speed. I search for reputable charities so I can offload my disgustingly amassed fortune. The first search result is a religious charity that helps children, and the needy. I click faster than I ever have; a fanatical feeling pushes its way into my mind. I click on the link and read the words at the top of the website:

> The way you get meaning into your life is to devote yourself to loving others, devote yourself to your community around you, and devote yourself to creating something that gives you purpose and meaning.
> —Mitch Albom

My eyes immediately well up. I've spent my whole life doing nothing but using the goodwill and trusting natures of others for personal gain. That's why I could never find meaning, my cynicism and my hatred. Instead of making me happy, and allowing me to be successful, perhaps my cancer, was always part of my journey, a way to truly find the meaning I've been missing in my life.

I know what I have to do to finally feel like my life has true meaning. Is this for Zach Jr.? Am I replacing the piece in my heart that went missing during my sick past? Where was this compassion when I left my son all alone, after his mother, my wife died? Where was it when I was conning my way through life, without a care for anyone but myself? God somehow has gotten through to me, after all these years.

I find the donate button on the website and dump every account in the charity. I believe that this has been my destiny for quite some time, and God has let me to the right place. However, my days are numbered, my headaches and blurry vision get more and more frequent every single hour. I know that this will be the death of me, without question. I even keeled over in pain in front of Zach Jr., clutching my head and letting out a brief groan to express the horrifying pulsating that was shutting down my mind beat by beat.

My bank accounts are finally tapped; my sickness has been released. The slave who would do anything for money has become a free man. I once was an addict, a pervert, who was willing to go outside of his own nature and to destroy lives just to get ahead. I always had the intellect to make an honest living, but taking advantage of people satisfied some diseased and hidden part of my psyche. I hear my son calling from the other room and immediately close all the tabs in my browser. If he sees what I am doing, that could blow my cover and force me to tell him the truth in a way I have never intended.

I get up and walk into the kitchen, where Zach Jr. huddles over the stove. I ask what he is doing, and he replies with a smile, "I'm making us dinner. What does it look like?" As I stumble into the kitchen, my head pounds more and more. I try to push through, but my legs give out.

I immediately sit down in a chair to try and hide my illness from Zack. He looks at me with worry and asks, "Dad are you okay?"

I try to brush it off, saying, "Yes, of course. I'm fine."

He asks, "Dad, can you stir this for me? I need to go the bathroom." I muster the strength to stand up go to the stove. I look down at my hands and realize I can hardly see. I finally find the spoon after many seconds of awkward fishing around. Suddenly everything goes completely black, and I hit the floor.

CHAPTER 19

I awake with my fuzzy vision made worse by the overwhelming light shining into my eyes; it immediately forces me to close them again. I slowly flutter them open and shut to try and adjust to the light that is hitting them so abruptly. My eyes adjust after nearly a minute of quickly opening and closing them. I look around and realize where I am. I see something coming out of my arm, an IV, and also hear the beeping of the heart monitor. I think to myself, *At least I'm alive, at least I can still tell Zach Jr. the truth.* My head aches horribly, and my body feels weak and brittle. I send my eyes around the room looking for a sign of how long I've been here. I see a fresh bouquet of flowers, a sign that I must not have been out for long, or they would have wilted. Or someone would have taken them out of my room when they became a symbol for death and no longer one of life and love. I look down at my lap and see a white sheet of paper; maybe it has information about how long I've been here? I attempt to grab the paper but immediately become dizzy and out of breath. My strength is being sucked out of me by the second. I have never felt a weakness like this in my life. I feel as if I can't move at all. I keep trying to grab the piece of paper; it is like a prize. I long for the information it may contain that says what happened to me. Eventually, I develop a strategy to slowly walk my hands down to the paper, which allows me to use the strength still left in my fingers. I finally reach the note, after a struggle that seems appropriate for someone trying to break a world record in weightlifting.

I grip the paper firmly and quickly shove it up to my face, trying to read it with my blurred vision. I struggle with the words and letters, piecing together what the note said, much like a small child beginning to read.

———————⚫◆◆⚫———————

Dear Dad,

Thank you for everything you've done for me these past years, I have loved every moment we've spent together. You're truly an inspiration to me, and the one person I look up to.

However, Dad, I know. I know the truth; I know about your fame, the wonderful books you wrote, your past—everything you've hidden from me. I understand. I know why you didn't want me to know, I'm not upset; I'm not angry. I've read every book, and they're amazing; they have an indescribable quality that I've not seen in other books. I feel as if I'm having a conversation with you, or even with myself, when I reading your books. When I didn't have you around me, I would read your books. I thought they would help me get to know my fathers. And they did, Dad. I learned how to love you, how to forgive you, by seeing the man you truly were. The fact that we didn't spend more time together breaks my heart, I knew something was not right. I could tell that you were not feeling well, and that it was more serious than a cold or the flu. I didn't tell you because I knew it would kill you to know. I've struggled over telling you this for many years. I'm sure you had a hard time knowing whether to tell me or not as well. Thank you for everything you've done for me. I love you, Dad.

Love,
Zach

I cry as I finished the last words of the letter; "I love you, Dad" rings in my head like a bell. He knew, the entire time, the truth about his father. We both went through the same internal struggle over to tell the other. Surprisingly a sense of peace washed over me, and all the urgency and stress were flushed out of my body. The weight that had crushed me for so long was gone. I could finally live freely, and yet my life was being taken away from me. God gave me peace before my death, however. I knew that this was part of his plan; every decision in my life, every wrong or right turn, placed me right here. I had no regrets anymore, because I had finally found the meaning I had been searching for, the meaning of the life of Zach Smith.

I sit in my room alone pondering my many great triumphs and failures. I hope that eventually Zach Jr. will join me. He is the only thing I have in the world and I greatly wish to see him before my time on earth expires. I am now free of guilt, a completely new man; however my end is approaching quickly. I hear the doorknob jiggling and voices outside the door. I assume a staff person is coming to check on me or bring me a meal. I have no idea what time it is. Much to my surprise, a group of people—clearly not doctors or nurses—walk into my room. I quickly say "I think you might have the wrong room." My voice is scratchy and dry, since I have not spoken for some time. However, as if God has given me his two eyes, my sight suddenly becomes clear as ever. I see my son, brother, mother, and sisters. I am stunned, in the most joyous of ways, unable to believe these people I love so much have come together for me after all this time. After everything, every mistake, they have forgiven me. Everyone huddles around my bed n silence. I look at them and ask, "Why?" I whisper to stifle my tears. They all call out at once: "Because we love you." How have I been so blind. My cynicism and my arrogance led me to push away everyone who was close to me. I assumed they hated me or despised me. Maybe I hated myself. This sick perception I created; was it wrong all this time?

I talk to my family for a short while before my head starts to boil. I can feel my life being sucked out of me yet again, and my

God-given eyesight is being taken me from me. I ask everyone to let me and my son have the room to ourselves for a short while. They oblige and promptly leave. I look up with a smile and say, "So the cat's out of the bag huh?" I chuckle softly, my chest aching with each rising laugh.

He smiles as well and says, "It's okay, Dad, I loved the books, every word helped me reach you, and learn about you. You don't have to feel guilty anymore."

The smile drops from my face like a boulder off the side of a cliff. "Zach Jr. don't believe a word in those books, ever. Don't be a fool the way I was. Don't doubt what should not be doubted, and don't assault yourself the way I assaulted myself. You are only sixteen years old, and you have your whole life ahead of you, even if that means living without me," A tear falls from my eye. "And most of all, do not let vanity blind you into creating something evil, as I did. Do not let vanity get the best of you and make you believe there is no God. God is real. There is a greater power, and it is not our own intelligence. God is here this very moment watching over us. Please, son, if you want to honor me in death—I am pleading with you on my death bed—then learn to love God. Learn how to be a better man than I was. I shouldn't be your role model; I did everything the wrong way. I never accepted God; I didn't want to feel like someone was guiding my journey. Now I realize that your journey is what you make of it. If you help others and resist the greed and lust that plague us all, then you will be so much happier for it. Zach, don't be like me; be better."

Zach looks at me as I sit in my hospital bed, withering away. "How can you love God?" he asks. "He put you on a path that led to your untimely demise."

"This disease has brought me more happiness than anything else in my life," I reply. "It brought us all together. It gave my life meaning. It got every secret, every lie out in the forefront."

Zach Jr. tries to hold back tears but ultimately lets a few slip. "I just wish he wasn't taking you now that we're happy," he says. "But yes, I do believe in him. Yes, I do love him. And every word you have just told me right now, I will cherish and abide by for the rest of my life. I will listen to you and become a good man just like you are, even though you may not see it."

"Zach, you will be led somewhere great," I say quickly. "I see more genius in you than I ever had. Be kind, be a leader, be better man than I was. And remember this: if you are anything like me, you will one day realize that only you can break yourself; others cannot break you. You are very strong yet so vulnerable to your own thoughts and view of yourself. Don't ruin your view of yourself because that is something you can get back."

My voice grows weaker; my brain feels as if it is descending into a realm of peace. This is the end as I know it. It is as if my earthly voice is coming to an end. I stare into Zach's eyes and say, "I love you to death, and please tell the rest of the family that I love them to death. Peace to you, Zach." I look up at him and the last things I see are his eyes crying a river. I look down and using everything I have left in my final breath, I utter in Arabic, "To God we belong, and to him we shall return."

I scream. I pant. I run around in circles like a dog chasing his own tail. His death has jumpstarted my life. Now I chase a ghost who was ever so great, ever so intelligent, oblivious to the hatred around him. In fact, that hatred never truly existed; the only genuine hatred was his hatred for himself. Now I chase a ghost that resides on top of the world, who lives in my head day and night, and tries to get me to do everything I can to suppress his ignorant fan base that resides in this world. Now I chase a ghost with the intent of dethroning him, killing off all he ever was, because he was too soft, too unworthy of the control he had. I will let my intelligence dictate my path, but I won't fall in the same trap of the ghost I am chasing. I will outdo him in everything, because I am greatness and superior to all. I will chase the ghost until he no longer has a name. And the name of that ghost is Zach Smith, my father. Now Dad, try and tell me not to be who you were. You're nothing but a corpse, and now I will become the man you feared all this time I will become … Zach Smith Jr.

Printed in the United States
By Bookmasters